STEPHEN P. BURNS

FINN'S DESTINY: THE HAND OF FATE

This be the Second Edition, Published 2010.

ISBN1449903185
EAN-139781449903183

Category: Fiction / Fantasy / General

Printed in the USA

Dedicated to

Maria, Ruarí & Robin

My inspiration.

Before

Finn McGarrigle watched intently as his brother Dara deftly flicked the spinning soccer ball with a sleight of foot that was both artful and masterful. At the same time he was dodging the burly youths bearing down on him from two directions, by simply stepping out of their way as they proceeded to collide with each other. Then, twisting with grace and not a little skill, Finn had to admit, Dara kicked the ball squarely into the back of the net, apparently without a trace of effort or the arrogance normally associated with football heroes. He smiled and winked over to his brother on the sides, and gave his closest teammate a high five.

Finn punched the air with joy as the ball hit the net. He would have leapt off the ground, had he the ability. However, he remained fixed to the spot. He was proud of his brother's skill and obvious athletic ability and his popularity…and his legs. But he hated him too, and he hated himself for hating him and the things he could do. Only eleven months younger than Finn, Dara was the most popular kid in his year. He was strong, tall and good looking, and he was always out there running or walking, or talking and getting on with a life that Finn could only dream of. Like his brother, Finn had been tall and strong. Finn looked at his useless legs and thought of the promise he had shown, before it was all taken away. He remembered how he had been the skilled one, how he was Captain of the team, and how he had the life. But not now…

At 17 he was a shadow of his former self; broken and useless, dour and unpopular. He was envious of the others going their own way living an independent life in ways he felt he never, ever would again. His supposed friends were all going out at night, or having fun with girlfriends. He had to wait for his Dad to take him out, or drop him at the club, or at the school, where they all felt sorry for him. Finn had enough self pity to last a century. He didn't need their pity. Girls would come and talk to him, but they always looked down on him. Well, they couldn't help it, could they? He was only four feet tall now, sitting in this contraption.

He was awakened from this drift into misery as his energetic bright brother bounded in front of him, grinning inanely.

"I think that'll clinch it, don't you?" he beamed. "Only ten minutes to go." And he bounced off, a bundle of teenage energy, as the local girls fawned over him, whistling and cheering wildly.

"Yeah, I'm sure it will," Finn said, quietly but sourly. Instantly he loathed himself for thinking that way. Dara wasn't to blame, he had to keep reminding himself. He sometimes thought that it must be difficult for him, too. Dara had to drag him about often enough. He had to include him in things he did. That must really make his day. Finn was the older brother, but Dara was his babysitter.

He thought about his condition all the time and it had soured him. He had been outgoing, full of life, and a bit of a tearaway. He had even been in some real trouble …but only because he was caught. It was joyful, boyish fun. He had his mates and he had his independence; he could do what he wanted. But those days were all gone. He was robbed of his youth, and now he felt like he was a tired and miserable old man, sitting on his backside all day, looking forward to a future of sitting on that backside in an office, probably tied to some computer terminal. He would be the computer and that move would cement his descent from humanity.

But it wasn't Dara's fault. It wasn't Dad's fault. There was no one here to blame, but that didn't stop him. There was really only the rotting body of a nameless drunk, dragged from his burning car and buried three years ago, on the same day as Finn's Mum.

Only Finn hadn't known that. He hadn't known his Mum was dead. They didn't tell him and he couldn't be aware, anyway. He hated them all for that.

"*We can't upset him, not just now,*" Finn had heard the tiny, distant whispers through the bandages and the pain, and above the noise of the machines beeping beside his head.

"*He needs to heal first…. it might put him back into…* " And the voices faded into indecipherable technical jargon.

"*Shhhh, Dara…leave your brother to sleep…he needs time.*"

He had felt time intensely, as though he owned it. Minutes could pass but they would seem like years. He did not really know how long he had been there, but the voices drifted back and forth all the time. Sometimes they were familiar, sometimes they weren't….

It had been late at night, and they were all returning from a great holiday. The Ferry had been running late. It was a long tiring day. It had been raining, but that didn't matter. A great time had been had, but now it was time to go home. That was fine. Back home to your own things. Back to your room, to your computer, and your own games. Back to your friends with whom you would be hanging out tomorrow, getting back to real life.

Sitting comfortably and languishing in boredom in the back seat of their bright red Volvo V70 station wagon he had drifted into sleep, and only awoke as the car swerved violently. It seemed to be spinning and so was his head. The screech of brakes and the screams of his family all around him...Then, it was real chaos as the other car, coming from the other direction and wildly out of control, travelling much too fast, was crossing the central reservation. He had seen the two bright headlights blindingly close. Then, it hit their car head on. With the impact, their car had come to a sudden and complete halt, but the luggage, stacked clumsily and untidily in the open boot space the previous night in a great rush before that last precious bottle of French Red, kept moving with the power of its own inertia. It flew around their heads as if in slow motion or in space. He could remember thinking he would be safe. He was wearing his seat belt; he had done everything correctly. He was awake and aware now.

"Hold on and you'll be fine," he had thought. "I've been good, really. I'm not going to die." He couldn't feel anything so he couldn't be hurt, there were voices all around so everyone else had to be safe, too.

The noise was ferocious as the other car spun on, hitting the bridge parapet and flying into space. And then there was the silence, apart from the distant rumble of the other traffic approaching from afar to greet the horrors that waited. Finn had looked around before feeling the real intensity of the pain in his legs and his face, and the blackness; the scary dark void came. Then all was quiet and after that it was the pain and the voices... and later still the biggest pain.

He hadn't been well enough to leave the hospital for the funeral, and everyone was of a consensus it '*wouldn't be a good thing.*' Anyway, no one asked for his opinion, and no-one ever would now. After that there was the physiotherapy and the surgery and the pain. He ended up looking like an unfinished freak. Well, so he thought…

"I ate through a straw for a whole year, for Gods sake," he thought, self piteously.

Hard suitcases might be a great thing when your luggage is roughly manhandled as it progresses through an airport, but it isn't so good when it goes through your face, he had thought, darkly. And the legs. Who needs legs when you can have wheels?

And now, he felt like he was a burden to Dad and to Dara. They had their crosses to bear; their tearful quiet moments, and they lugged him about all over the place. What a life.

Frreeeeeeeeepppp!!!! The final whistle sounded and he woke, startled, from his nightmare. Dara ran over and shouted something about winning, again. Finn shook himself from the gloom and felt genuinely pleased, and he smiled.

"I'll be over in ten minutes. Don't run away. " Dara joked.

"Ha… ha …ha." Finn felt it. "He just doesn't think sometimes, but then why should he?"

Sitting around was part of life now, and the time passed as it always did…slowly. At least his hands worked and the games console he carried about helped to pass it. Dara soon appeared in the distance, laughing and joking with an ease that Finn envied, with two girls cooing over him. He began to push the wheelchair.

Finn joked feebly about always being pushed around, but soon their conversation turned to the game and the possibility of actually bringing home the cup, and to the two girls, and then laughter and fun came back into his life, just as it usually did when he was alone with his brother. All the horrible thoughts dissipated in his company, and the envy and the jealousy and all that vanished. They were the best of friends.

Neither of them noticed the car approaching from behind. There was blaring music, open windows, and idiots leaning out shouting abuse at the passers-by. Soon it was evident though as it passed them, and again time began to slow. They both looked round as the full Coke can flew through the air, fizzy dark fluid spilling from it in a hyperbolic arc, and retaining the momentum of the moving car. It hit Dara firmly on the side of his head. He raised his hands as the pain surged through it and the wheel chair slipped out of his grasp. At first it seemed hugely funny to Finn, but then it wasn't….

Finn tried to slow himself, but in the panic his clumsy fingers couldn't get the brakes to work, and the friction from the growing speed of the wheels burned, and he had to let go. He steadily picked up speed, looking frantically around and panicking, looking for Dara to help him stop. He couldn't see him though, and Dara didn't help. Picking up speed he slew down hill. He was a speeding skier, weaving and twisting, fearing he might overturn and do himself some real damage; people saw this accident in motion, but no-one tried to help.

Instead they seemed to laugh as he sped past.

"Got your go-faster stripes?" He heard one shout out, but as this idiot disappeared in the moving throng, the realisation of where he was heading dawned and the fear came back. This path led directly to the Lang Steps; steep never ending hard concrete steps leading to oblivion.

He skidded and hit the top of the steps square on, trying as hard as he could to grab the central handrail, but it was no use. It slipped from his hands and he flew into space, still attached to the wheelchair as the momentum took it with him. As he went, he noticed the face of an old wizened man, bearded and bent, smiling serenely at him as he flew by. The old man winked, cocking his head slightly, still smiling. This tempered Finn's fear, giving him something else to think about and he was thankful he hadn't hit him. He closed his eyes and waited for the crash, the pain and the return to mangled, broken bones. All noise subsided and time slowed, and he was in the void again. The wind whistled around his head and he tightened his eyes praying for help, for a miracle to stop him hitting the hard concrete steps or the hard metal railing or, in fact, anything.... and then he came to a sudden halt. But this wasn't what he expected. There was no bone crunching pain, no tangle of wheelchair wrapping round his useless limbs, no screaming.

Instead, the landing was soft, if a bit scratchy, as he landed solidly on the moist, turfy earth of a forest floor. He opened his eyes slightly to see, and was blinded momentarily by the sunlight. Before he had time to think a voice full of laughter urged him to get up.

"Have you fallen off that horse again?" It was his brother, Dara.

And another thing, without even thinking, he had got back up onto his legs.

1 The Homeland

Finn gathered himself up, and looked around at the unfamiliar surroundings. His head twisted frantically. He looked around this way, then that, and then more slowly he took in the breathtaking beauty of this forest, with its lush greenery and the dappled sunlight of a hot summers day falling through the whispering leaves of the forest canopy. A dry comfortable heat permeated the air.

A host of insects flitted chaotically through the leaves, and filled the forest with teeming life. Every so often a wildly colourful bird would swoop down from the heights grabbing a huge dragonfly in its beak, or making an eerie, but strangely welcoming, screeching sound. The floor of the forest was covered in an immense purple sea of bluebells and they made a beautiful soft carpet under his newly discovered feet, now wrapped in sackcloth, with leather thongs retaining the cloth in place.

Peace was on the earth and he could feel it in his very bones, and in those legs that had been useless for these three interminable years. He felt like he was, for want of a better word that might express the wholeness of this situation, Home.

Heat flowed through his legs as he stood unsteadily, fearing he might collapse at any moment, but knowing intrinsically he could do anything; he could run, he could jump, he could even just walk if that's what he wanted. He could ride his mountain bike, useless for all those years and gathering dust in the shed, through these trails, if in fact bikes existed here. The adrenalin rush from this realization made him feel invincible, and a surge of emotion flowed through his chest, leaving him exhilarated and then drained at the same time. Without realising it he was dancing around in some sort of primitive, made up Irish jig. He had even kicked his heels as he jumped around.

Through the dappled leaves he felt the warm friendly sunlight on his face and put up his hands to the broken cheeks and the scarred face. The skin was smooth and young feeling and the pain was gone. The blind spot caused by his lost eye was whole again and his distance vision and perception of depth had returned. He was whole again…but how?

But then he thought, panicking, of the fall and what had happened. His mind whirled in a rush of different emotions. What was going on? Then the questions fell over each other. Where am I? Who am I? Why has this happened? What has happened? Am I still at home? Am I alive? Or is this simply heaven? If so, it was the epitome of heaven. Emotions rushed through his head, and he fell to his knees on the soft ground, with the contradictions flying in violent circles around his confused brain, now growing fuzzy with the myriad of different signals coming into it.

"Have you knocked your head on a branch or something?" The voice was saying. "Are you alright? We have been looking for you for hours…you look …a bit strange…what's going on?"

"I was hoping you might tell me that." He heard himself answering.

Surprisingly, the impediment caused by his missing piece of tongue, bitten off in the accident and seemingly irreplaceable, was gone and he rolled this new tongue, no, his old tongue, around in the cavern of his mouth, touching the ridges in the roof with the now sensitive tip and feeling for his full set of teeth with the relish of a great discovery. Whole indeed, and with the warm glow of satisfaction coursing through his veins he looked round to see the owner of the voice.

This was his brother, Dara, fresh faced and bright, sitting high up on a horse. He was different though; a little less sure of himself, Finn could tell, and his worried, no… concerned, expression was tell tale that he had a respect for Finn, not the old, shrugging air of obligation he had before. Something else was different here then, Finn thought. Finn knew instinctively that here, he was the older brother, not just some burden to be carried until Dad said he could go and mess about with his own friends. No obligation, no carrying, no simmering resentment.

He bit on his lip as he surveyed the scene. He looked at the strange new clothes he was now wearing. Brown serge trousers, sackcloth shirt, cloth boots, and a cloak. Where did these come from?

"Something's happened, " Finn said, " and I don't know where I am…or, where this forest …is." He let the phrase hang in the silence of the forest glade, hoping for an instant answer to explain it all, which he knew he would not get.

"East of the sun and west of the moons, old Finn," his brother said, laughing. Finn hadn't the faintest idea what he was talking about. "We'd better get you home, and quick. Everyone is out looking for you. They're all worried, and now you seem…a bit stranger than usual. I have to get you home right now. Can you mount your horse or should I go and get some help? The footmen could help get you back, but you don't seem to need any physical help…. Do you think you're all right? Do you need to see that old quack, Squeller, again?"

"Who?" Finn thought abstractedly, looking at the new surroundings. " Err…. I really don't know where this is."," and he became aware he sounded a little panicky now.

"You're only in the Forest. You know… The Kernels…The forest? You know that, don't you? We're only about five miles from home, but you seemed to have disappeared completely, we've been looking for hours. We thought you might have been trying to get through the forest to the Wastelands again, perhaps. On another foolish quest? You know we are not allowed to go there again. You might have been attacked by the ……never mind… you seem basically all right, and you're safe now at least. Come on, Let's get you home and call off the rest of them."

Finn looked over now at the giant beast at the other side of the clearing, standing patiently, its reins dangling, chewing lazily on clumps of lush green grass. He hadn't been aware of it until now, and Dara was expecting him to ride it home. Seventeen hands. How did he know that?

With unsteady legs he walked towards it with a feeling of trepidation. How do I get seventeen hands into the air and onto its back? But, holding the reins in his hands a quiet knowledge came over him and he pulled himself effortlessly onto the saddle with an uncomplicated ease, as if from experience gained over many years and forming an instinctive ability. This felt odd, but at the same time totally natural. He and this beast were one. No more metal, no more wheels, no more four feet tall…he strode the world ten feet from the ground and felt the powerful surge of energy, the adrenalin, rush through his chest and his head and his legs. And with a kick, he was off.........

"Slow down!...No wonder you banged your head. You can't rush through the forest like this! It's just not safe to...." Dara's voice trailed off into the distance behind him as his mount sped through obviously familiar territory. This was totally new to Finn, but he was exhilarated by the speed, the rushing wind at his heels, and the exotic smells of this forest. With his head low against the powerful beast, he could do anything. If he *had* died, so what, he wanted to make the most of it.

2 *Home*

Soon the forest thinned and then cleared, and he saw as he slowed up that he was in a meadow of yellow flowers on the outskirts of a sprawling, mediaeval looking town. A narrow and straight, compacted dirt track led through the straggling mass of ramshackle houses, but he could see ahead that the buildings became denser, and rose on what appeared to be a conical mountain to a Castle high above and dead centre of the town. The houses seemed to be rising up to meet it; to get closer if they could, perhaps to bask in the Castle's glory.

And glorious a sight it was too. Its parapets and high imposing warm honey sandstone walls looked strong and safe. These outer walls were squarely built, and had a satisfying, subtle and perfect ratio of length to height, which was absolutely aesthetically pleasing. To someone who appreciated geometry and the perfection in mathematics, its physical realisation in the architecture here made this structure seem perfect. It was, in a word, Castle-ly, if that actually was a word. But it certainly fitted this one. At regular intervals there were voids in the walls, tall windows, each with the same ratio of height to width.

He could see that there was a walkway with a parapet on the top of the walls and tiny figures could be discerned, patrolling. Inside the walls was a massive gleaming white structure, tiered, with many narrow towers of varying height, which rose erratically and seemingly randomly, as if organically grown from the inner sanctum. Each was topped with a steeply sloping conical roof, slated in a pleasant terracotta stone. Some towers were upright and proud, but some seemed to droop and bend, almost groaning, under an unseen weight towards the courtyard.

In the centre was a single enormous domed roof, green with patina, and itself topped with a pointed observation tower, perched impossibly, teetering on the brink of falling, from which a lengthy telescope could be seen glinting in the pale evening sunlight. It could have been Camelot. But it wasn't; this was real. But it was also so perfect. Somehow, Finn had gathered that this was home. Dara caught up, panting.

"You…. are an idiot," he said, laughing loudly, and he slapped Finn hard on the back as they headed into the town. They still had the same connection. As if from nowhere, at that moment, they were joined by two menacing men in matching armour, with chain mail heavier than Finn could have imagined it possible to carry, and each sporting an array of weaponry that made him wince at the thought of the pain they could inflict. They remained silent but rode ahead of them, clearing the way through the town.

Dara commented, "They're thick as two short planks this two. How are they to protect us if anything happens? I think that even The Fools could outwit them."

The streets of the town were filling with people now, but as the guards passed through they parted and reverently let the small entourage past. Some bowed; some touched their foreheads, respectfully. Finn gaped at them.

"Can't be too careful these days," Dara said quietly.

" Was a time we could have been here alone, but not now…I don't know what you were thinking about. Come on, let's get home before the moons are out."

"Croí Dorchadas; that's where we are heading. The Heart of Darkness," Dara informed him. He must have expected Finn to know this fact, but he obviously liked playing with the menacing phrase.

"They couldn't have named it better all those centuries ago if they tried. Don't you think? It must have meant, or been something else then, though. What do you think," and he rolled it about again, "…the Heart of Darkness, is?"

After a few more minutes contemplation he said to Finn, "You do realize the trouble you are in now, don't you? The Guardian won't stand for it. I should know, shouldn't I? Got away with it the last time by the skin of my teeth. Still, you're the special one aren't you? The sun shines out of your backside. They might be listening in. Bit dim, but they are able to commit exactly what you say to memory and might repeat it somewhere I'd rather they didn't."

They rode silently now through the evening air. It was warm and very pleasant and the surrounding scene was incredibly interesting. The streets of the town were bustling with energy and life; children playing, old men arguing over a game which involved throwing round pebbles into a chalked circle in which there was an egg waiting to be smashed. Women were carrying baskets of exotic fruits and strangely shaped and coloured vegetables, and chickens squawking angrily as they were chased along the street and then suddenly turning on the dogs, who took flight and ran as they saw their vicious teeth…

"What's that there?" Finn asked, pointing at a tall wooden structure on the horizon.

Dara wrinkled his nose, frowning, and looked at Finn as though he was mad.

"That's Old Cyrill's boat, of course. It's enormous. That must be at least two whole miles away. He'll save us all from the rain. He's totally mad. It's coming, soon he says, …ooooohhh!" Dara put on a screechy awestruck voice. "… And we will all perish if we don't watch out and mend our rotten ways."

"There isn't even a river nearby so how's he going to float it?" Dara said, back in his own voice. "Anyway, why d'you ask, now? You were the one who was ridiculing him about it, last week …You went up to him and told him to his face he was completely insane, that it would never happen, that the sky just wouldn't fall in …mind you the Guards were there to back you up and save your skin if he tried to bite you, or something like that."

He continued, "My friends hear their parents repeat all the rubbish they talk about him in the chambers. That he is some sort of prophet. Two years ago, he decided a flood would erupt from both the earth and the skies, following a long period of drought. And believe it or not, he claims he can prove it is coming by using ancient runes of course, and some frighteningly portentous omens. Of course, they are completely made up…. So, the weather has admittedly been drier than of recent years. So there it is. A bit of a folly, but people come from near and far to see it and to listen to him prattle on."

Finn thought for a moment and said, "I seem to have forgotten an awful lot, somehow. What has happened to me? And you say I was gone for only a few hours?" He was puzzled about this trivia, which he clearly should have known.

"Well…it's not the first time," Dara said matter of factly. " You had a weird sleeping sickness, some years ago. Lost your memory then too, but it all came back. I had to help. The Guardian got some old witch in to wave her hand about and sprinkle cockerel feathers or rat dung or something else over you, and about a week later you woke up mumbling about your legs being numb and your face being sore." He put his hands up to his face and rolled his eyes skywards, and again in a high pitched voice acted out his brother's tragic pleas.

"I thought you were just making it up at first for a bit of fun, but then it just lasted too long."

"Anyway after some time you were normal and back at your place on the Table. We kind of expect some emergency or drama every now and then from you…. And you always provide it, just on cue. What kind of King are you going to make, though; disappearing half the time, not remembering anything the next? I could just pretend you're a servant next time."

By now, they were climbing the hill towards the Castle. Steeply inclined houses lined the street, each identical, in rows, now constructed of stone with ornate doors and ironwork, each one louder than the last. Then the houses spread out and each had a small courtyard. The obvious effect was that each tried to out-do the last in a mutually assured, destructive way, with more and more money being spent on each house as they got closer to the Castle. They were soon totally spread out, in an organic, random layout as though they had grown from seeds thrown out of the looming Castle. Ostentation was reeking from the doors and windows, with greater and greater vulgarity in the hideous adornments. Then there was nothing but empty space, and the Castle entrance, far ahead across a cobbled courtyard where fireflies the size of mice fluttered happily in the twilight glow of the two pallid moons.

3 *The Castle*

As they entered the grounds, Finn stretched his head back and looked upwards at the tall towers of the Castle and tried to see to the top. They seemed to disappear impossibly into the darkening sky, so he gave up. What he did notice were two enormous ravens perched high up on the parapets, squabbling. In the yellow flickering firelight from the braziers in the courtyard he could tell they were metallic blue in colour and must have had a seven-foot wingspan. He hoped that was the case, because if they were any further away, they would be unfeasibly large and a bit too scary for his liking.

As they reached the immense wooden doors, two courtiers scurried out of the shadows and took the reins of the horses. Finn and Dara dismounted and walked up the impressive stone steps to the doors. Finn turned to look round, and the horses had gone, all the guards had gone, and they were alone in the extensive open courtyard.

He turned back to look at the doors. They were constructed of huge rough timber planks, which were held together with blackened iron rivets; each one six full inches across at the head. The doors themselves were each at least forty feet high and ten feet across, and he wondered in a frivolous way, how he might reach the doorbell.

"No change there," he thought as he remembered, distastefully, that he couldn't reach it at home either, because they hadn't thought to move it down to a more suitable level for him. There was a horrible screeching, scraping sound, and a tiny door hidden in the immensity of the wooden doors opened, and a little old man looked out, dressed in brown sackcloth rags. He had loaves of bread in his hands, as if waiting to feed the enormous ravens.

In a thin, reedy, and tremulous old man's voice he hurried them in and quickly shut the tiny door behind him. He then spent a full five minutes closing various locks and bolts, opening some again and then closing them. Inside, a tall officious looking man dressed in a suit of black stretchy material which pulled over his rotund upper body as if it were a huge stocking, with loose straggly ends hanging from ragged sleeves, and a black skull cap which appeared to be, just, too big for him, was waiting. He waved his hands quickly and dismissively, shooing off the wizened old man, who wandered off as if dazed, shaking his head and muttering something about the price of bat feet not being what it was…

"Can't be too careful, " the official man said, smilingly, in an oily voice. " Better get in, quick. Now you pair go straight to your quarters and wait for the bell. A banquet is being prepared in honour of your return, young Sir

Finn, and we need to follow procedures, after all." Finn noticed the man wore a roughly hewn, stone name badge, pinned incongruously to his stretchy suit. "Percival," it said, in loud florid writing, on a swirling purple background. Percival noticed Finn looking at the badge and rubbed it with a ragged sleeve, proudly beaming.

"Awarded only today, for many, many years of dedicated loyal service," he said, gazing into the space ten metres ahead of him. " Imagine, a name of my own, at last...."

As they moved away and started to climb the steep wide stone stairs leading to their rooms, Dara said to Finn in a low whisper, "Hope you are not too hungry after your stupid adventures, Finn.... once we've followed procedure, it'll be tomorrow." The whisper seemed to echo throughout the cavernous hallway, and then it disappeared, only to come back to them from a window high above them in the tall, round turret.

"I heard that!" an oily voice reverberated from afar and around the hall. "Ritual is what makes life worth living!" the disembodied voice said.

Finn and Dara laughed conspiratorially and made their way up the stairs. After the first flight they had acquired a comfortable red carpet.

" I somehow don't know where to go," said Finn with a growing lack of confidence in his new exciting life. How could he pull this off? How could he get by if he had forgotten his life here? Did he have a life here, or was this a dream? If it was, he surmised, if he just let things happen, then it would all unfurl logically, or something like that. If it was a dream, then he knew everything anyway, as it was all in his own head, so why not relax and enjoy the ride…

He took heed of his own advice, took a deep breath and looked up at the unending stairs. He was exhausted and couldn't be bothered walking, and remarked to Dara that this seemed too far.

"You lazy turnip head!" Dara replied, and he held his arm out to bring them to a halt.

"Why not just use the right words?"

Dara announced out in a loud assertive voice, "Carpet; Move!" and underneath their feet the carpet began moving, carrying them slowly up to their place of rest. This was more like it, Finn thought, wide eyed and open mouthed; amazed at the magical ride. (Surreptitiously, Dara had only pulled a hidden lever he knew Finn must have forgotten about, and set in motion a mechanism that moved the carpet. He thought this was a smart trick, and he rarely had the opportunity to outwit his brother. He travelled up the stairs smiling quietly….)

After some minutes the stair carpet disgorged them onto a landing, which was lit, dimly, by a flaming torch. There were torches along each side of the corridor wall at a distance of some ten feet between each. Finn assumed there was a mirror at the end of the corridor, because the torches stretched out to infinity. But then he realised, they did…..

An endless array of solid wooden doors accompanied the torches, and the choice of rooms looked impossible, but he knew that the first door he looked at would be the right one. And it was. He reached to open it, but knocked loudly on it first, not expecting there was anyone in there, but to see if it made a sound, and what sound it might be, and how loud. It echoed, too, into the distance. Dara left him and walked another ten paces to the next door, and opened it, looking over at him quizzically.

"You're sure you are all right? " Dara asked slowly.

"Yeah I'm fine," said Finn dreamily; as sure as he could be that he was.

"Look," he said trying to get his thoughts in order. "Things seem a bit, well, different to me just now. Like in a dream. I can't really explain, not just yet, but I might try later. You just won't believe me when I… oh forget it, just now."

Dara looked puzzled, " I'll just get out of this stuff and come to your room for you in a minute, OK?"

Finn opened his door and walked into the room. The fact he was walking had only been in the back of his mind, but now on his own he became hyper-aware of the use of his legs. This was the most fantastic thing. He told himself; again, this must be an hallucination, so as not to get too excited by it. He might be dead now, or in the next few instances, for all he really knew, so what use would they be then?

Looking in the door, he expected something breathtaking, but it seemed ordinary, uncomplicated, even rustic. It was a large, well-spaced room, however, as he had totally expected in a Palace, with a large comfortable bed in the centre and various pieces of utilitarian wooden furniture; wardrobes, chests, a table, some chairs and a desk. There was no visible lighting, but the bare, stone walls were illuminated with a subtle ethereal, almost daylight, almost twilight aura. He noticed that the light seemed to brighten wherever he was, to illuminate the local area, totally. He could see an enormous open window that must look out onto the open courtyard, and he caught a glimpse of the moon, or more accurately one of the moons, out of it through the flimsy gossamer curtains that hung unsupported from the wall above it.As he looked around he could see the walls were not bare, as he had thought, but each lit area had a painting, or a tapestry, or a mirror, or some bizarre looking object indescribable to Finn's understanding. Some appeared to reverberate and change form as you looked past them. And he was aware that as he looked round the artefact disappeared from his peripheral vision, as if it wasn't there at all.

On the table there was a highly ornate glass jug, decorated with strange etched symbols. It was filled with water, and realising his thirst he launched straight into it. The jug was lighter than he expected and it almost flew upward out of his hands. Gaining full control of it, he poured the water into a goblet, sitting next to the jug. The goblet was so fine it was practically non-existent. He took a deep, deep draught. The taste was spectacular. This wasn't water, or at least not ordinary water. He couldn't quite grasp what it tasted of, but each mouthful was an amazing surprise, different each time. Thirst thoroughly slaked, he carefully placed the goblet on the marbled table, as lightly as he could for fear of breaking it. When he looked at it again, it had refilled. He picked it up again, puzzling over this feat, and walked over to the window.

The moons lit the courtyard with a ghostly midnight glow, and he could see that there was some life out there. The Fireflies were still there, fluttering blithely and aimlessly, it appeared, and sometimes fluttering right into the Castle walls, sometimes extinguishing themselves on the braziers. A black cat with two tails scurried across the cobbles and squealed loudly.

Two guards at the distant gatepost could be heard chatting and coughing, and he could see their breath as though it was a cold frosty night. Perhaps, it was over there, for it was so far away.

Then he became aware of something else moving slowly in the shadows. At first he thought it was another cat, or a dog or some other creature, but he soon became aware it was a girl. Her frame was very small and she had spindly, thin limbs. Her hair was obviously very long and seemed straggly and unkempt. He could see her face now, and it was thin and elfin, pointed at the cheeks and the chin, and there were shadows cast by her cheeks that elongated her face and made her eyes seem sad and sunken. She was wearing a short, sheer dress that was shimmering in the moonlight. It had a strange ethereal glow, quite out of place with the material. It seemed alive.

At first, he thought she had perhaps broken in and might be trying to steal something, but then he saw she carried a wrap, and as she rushed across the courtyard, unaware of her wide-eyed audience, she dropped something of its contents on the ground. It was a small round stone, the size of a new salad potato, and was radiating light, as if on fire. She bent down and quickly scooped it up, placing it in the wrap. It did not seem to be as hot as it looked from Finn's viewpoint.

And then she carried on her way. She was heading towards the doorway now, and it became difficult to see her. Finn was so entranced with this vision that he climbed right out of the open window onto a ledge, conveniently located at just the right height for him to carefully balance, but also hold on to the window frame at the same time. He was in place just in time to see her place each stone carefully into the fountain in the centre of the courtyard right outside the door. There was a hiss of steam, and a flash of light from each one and then they faded. The elfin girl danced slowly round in a circle, her arms outstretched, as though part of a circle of dancing friends… ring a ring a roses, we all fall down.

Finn was not to know she was accompanied, but then he couldn't be expected to be able to see everything in this land. Her back arched and her face looked up at the night sky past Finn on his window ledge, and she laughed loudly, smiling at the unseen group she frolicked with.

And then, as if from nowhere, the name *Enid* came into Finn's head in a whisper, and it flowed in circles through his mind as he savoured the name. Even though she was right in front of him, he shut his eyes to closely imagine the bearer of the name, and instantly she was there before him, seemingly in space, dancing by in slow motion, accompanied by swirling fairground organ music and glowing warmth, and in doing so missed her actually leave the courtyard, unseen by anyone.

There was a knock at the door, just loud enough to bring him out of his reverie. He shook and shivered, with the thoughts of *Enid* running through the courtyard, followed by an entourage of fanfares, horses, and flags; a saffron scarf billowing behind her, and glowing yellow in the twilight sun. She was gone.

As he opened the door to see Dara, he heard the echo from his experimental knock working its way back to its starting point. This could get a bit irritating, he thought as his dream was spoiled.

"I've got to go out!" he said, and he ran past Dara down the endless stairs towards the door. The wizened old man, Tremble, was there with his rack of keys slung round his neck on a chain. They were too heavy for his tiny frame to bear and he was bent double with the burden. His fingers moved rapidly around, shaking, on raised arms, and Finn realised with disappointment that he would never get the door open in time. He turned to see the obsequious Percival appear, as if on wheels. He rolled towards him and asked in his oozing way if there was anything wrong. Finn explained that he thought there was an intruder and Percival explained patiently that that could not be the case, for the security of this Castle ranked amongst the highest he knew of.

"Do you mean there is a drawbridge, or something like that, Percival?" Finn asked.

"Ah, you must be mistaken young sir, for I am not Percival, I am Pierre." He pointed at a badge, and there was a long silence as if Finn should say something apologetic, but he didn't, so Pierre continued; now in a French accent.

"Maintenant. To answer your question; do not worry yourself about trifles like that…there will be time enough when you are grown. Now, to your room until the Bell sounds. That is the signal. …One must always follow the ritual, or where would we all be?"

Finn felt he had no option and sulkily headed back up the steps, walking this time, his mind full of the spectre in ghostly white he had just observed. How would he see this vision again?

Half way up the stairs he was passed by a horde of gabbling, small men dressed in the ubiquitous black stretchy material, on their way down. They were tied together with a slim golden thread that slumped slackly between each as they moved in unison, without straining the cord. He couldn't understand a word they said, but they seemed to have purpose. He soon found out, as the bell he had waited for sounded, and the men each produced a tiny bell from their belts and joined in. The threads dissolved, and each headed off in a different direction along the nearest corridor and came to a halt outside a door, sounding their bells in an increasingly frantic and frenzied way. The bells were practically silent, and were in any case were drowned out by the main bell that echoed throughout the halls; its sound rebounding and resounding and setting up an interference pattern by itself with areas of calm amongst the heightened noise.

Then it stopped, and in unison all the doors opened and the halls were soon thronging with hundreds of people of all shapes, sizes, clothing, colours and hair styles. There was an excited chatter as they moved towards the stairs, and in a monolithic mass headed down the stairs. Finn was swept up with the crowd, all of whom smiled and nodded at him as they passed. Percival, Pierre, whoever he was, was at the foot of the stairs again and was passing out cards to each person as they passed. Strangely, though, he was also at the other side of the stairs, and also at the Massive door to the Banqueting Hall.

An army of identical Percivals were directing the crowd to the door and presumably to their tables inside. Finn walked up to the nearest, who smiled at him and said,

"Ahh….Master Finn, once more, do come inside, come through the door."

Realising he was incredibly hungry, he followed Percival's sound advice and entered the room. On entry, he expected this to be an enormous, beautifully decorated hall with long wooden tables populated by the likes of Henry VIII, ripping the legs of barely dead chickens and throwing bones over his shoulder; a jester would be entertaining, dressed in colourful rags with a tri-pointed hat with bells and carrying a wand with his own head on it, jousting mediaeval knights, sword fighting for the hand of a fair maiden…Anything could happen.

Instead, and to his deep surprise, not to say disappointment, he walked into a suburban semi detached house kitchen with a country cottage style table in the centre and embarrassingly ornate wooden chairs, each with a lace doily on the seat. As he looked back, he could still see the crowds in the great hall making their way into the doorway, but there they vanished, as if ghosts. Puzzled, he looked at Percival and shrugged. Percival came in and proffered a seat, pulling a chair out and inviting him to sit, grinning inanely.

"Master Dara will be here presently," he said, and exactly on cue Dara appeared.

"You were quick off the mark," he said.

"Why are we in our old kitchen at home?" Finn asked pointing around." Where's all the magic stuff."

"What do you mean?....This is home… and ..magic stuff?"

"Well… the majestic halls, the moving lights, ….the magic carpet for God's sake."

"And what's wrong with this? Who really wants to share their dinner with that lot?"

"Have you completely forgotten? It's all an illusion. Blink three times."

Finn did as he was told, and through shimmering air he saw that there was indeed an echoing banqueting hall, and everyone was seated and waiting for the meal to commence, chattering noisily about the price of gold and the unnatural weather they had recently had in a place far away…news of raindrops which shot sideways on landing and could flash up trouser legs if you were not careful, and all this after those months of dryness.

There appeared to be a thousand people in this hall, more than half of the town's population from Finn's quick guesstimate. Some must have come from further afield because the majority of the townsfolk must simply be too poor to attend such a banquet in this Castle. And, to emphasise this, there was the show of finery evident at each table, with each competing with their neighbour in exuberant displays of jewellery; or wearing wigs which reached impossibly for the rooftops; or with exotic cats on leads with diamond studded collars. Each table was, simply, worse than the next. It even extended to the cutlery they had brought with them.

Finn was at a long table, as he hoped, and was up on a dais; a stage above the rest of the throng. He sat at one end, and Dara at the other. In the middle was an outsized golden throne. Dara wondered aloud if 'He' would join us for the meal.

"Probably not; He hasn't for months."

Finn wondered who 'He' was. How big 'He' must be, considering the size of 'His' Throne. This was rather ominous. It couldn't be Dad by any chance? But, Dara would have said. He looked up and around at the hall which now impressed rather than disappointed him. It had a very high vaulted ceiling with spindly timber ribs holding up an impossibly high timbered roof. There was a clerestory of the bluest blue stained glass windows he had ever seen. Like St Chappelle in Paris, he remembered from a holiday some years ago, but even, if possible, bluer. It was absolutely beautiful.

High up in the airy vault, he could see an army of great grey owls blinking at each other with their weird spooky faces. There was a tiger chained on a stage near the centre of the room. A superb rose window was at one end of the hall, and above him, as he craned round to look at it, was a ceramic globe that swirled with a cloudy, wispy haze behind which an image of a real moon shone brightly. The crowd, who had also blinked three times, were 'oohing' and 'ahhing' as they went through a demonstration of the infinite phases of their moons, brought to them courtesy of a sun and two moons coinciding in the light and shadow of the Earth. Or might that be Earths?

The night's entertainment commenced with two funny Jesters, who wandered from table to table, cracking jokes and insulting the guests; all in good fun, of course. The crowd loved them, especially when they were the butt of the joke. There was clapping suddenly from the far end of the Hall, the lights dimmed and a shooting star shot across the face of the globe and from a void in the floor a squirming mass of the tiny men appeared bearing trays brim full of the most incredible food Finn had seen.

There were whole Boars roasted in wild garlic oils; small song birds skewered and roasted, with their own eggs as a side dish; potatoes suffused with oils; fruits Finn had never imagined, let alone seen; star fruits the size of footballs and strawberries coloured black with yellow leaves. In the centre of the table was a roasted pig's head, with a small roasted crow in its open jaw. Inside the crow's jaw was a single black olive.

The myriad of tiny hands brought forth plates, and all manner of strange cutlery for him to use. Finn had enough trouble coping with a knife and fork at home, so a fish-spoonknife could cause him major difficulties.

He tucked into whatever he fancied, and was soon enjoying game he would have turned his nose up at previously. Here, it just seemed normal to eat blood-encrusted slabs of meat and tough red coloured fowl. He had toyed with the idea of becoming vegetarian, just to annoy his Dad and to show what defiance he could in his normally helpless position, but that seemed far away now, and added to that, this feast changed his mind completely. Excitedly, he noticed he could taste sweet again after all these years, and he shouted out to Dara who looked at him askance, as if he were mad; not for the first time that day, of course.

As he ate he noticed the nearest tables float pleasantly aside from the centre of the hall. In a milky diffuse light, an orchestra appeared and began to play. Their instruments were metallic and bizarrely shaped, but the sound was extremely satisfying, creating a feeling of great depth in the listener's ears, but which ultimately led him to some lonely empty void when he closed his eyes. It was the closest he could get to imagining nothing. The ambient music was mesmerising, and soon Finn was lost in the deep, spacious sound they produced. The sound was bigger but also somehow sparser than anything he had heard before, and it infected his mind, expanding it and removing him from the Hall to an even more bizarre world. It was completely soporific.

For the second time tonight, though, he was rudely and abruptly awoken. The music suddenly stopped, the tiny men disappeared in their scurrying fashion, and the room dissolved. It was a bare stone walled barn of a room, and through the massive wooden doors at the head of the room, which had been flung open noisily reverberating through the hall, came the two brutish guards Finn had been escorted by earlier.

Between them they carried, rather dragged, the figure of a broken man, once tall and rangy, but now slumped and smashed. Percival wheeled up, his fingers moving together and apart nervously and quickly and he announced solemnly to the assembled crowd

"Ladies and Gentlemen, Lords and Ladies, Knights of the Realm, sirs and madams, and mademoiselles of course, I pronounce we have today captured our greatest foe, and we now bring him as tribute to our Lord and Great Master."

"To the great Guardian, who brings harmony to our Homeland, I present the prisoner and seditionist, Blaylock, finally captured entering the Homeland, complete with the evidence of devious plans for mass destruction. Please," and he puffed up his chest importantly " tell us your desires, Oh Lord and Master…"

He bowed with a great flourish, obviously highly satisfied with this his greatest achievement, and he looked directly into the eyes of Finn.

Finn gasped and was taken aback. He had originally thought this was like some theatrical event, for entertainment, but now it seemed that a life was in the balance and that he held the power of life over death. He hesitated, stammered and began to speak, but didn't know what or how to say anything. He fell silent, confused by the demand for action…

4 The Guardian

"That will be all."

A deep strong voice behind him had suddenly spoke up. Silently, someone had appeared at the throne at the centre of the table, as if materializing from nowhere. In an assertive, leading voice he said, "Take him to the Tower. Grindrod will deal with him, for now. I will be there presently." The broken figure was dragged away moaning in agony, and the jollity of the festivities took up again, as if nothing had interrupted them.

Finn realised he had been holding his breath and was almost choking, and he let it flood out in a stream of extreme relief. He turned round to look more closely at the owner of the voice. Tall and broad and dressed, of course, in black, but a black so dark it seemed to absorb all light from around it. Added to all this blackness was a voluminous, velvety cloak, which seemed to move freely and autonomously in the air around it, making its bearer seem much larger, and also strangely elusive. He had greying short hair, a fine face, pointed, with a small goatee type beard. Finn couldn't help but notice that the beard was blackened, and there was a small fingertip sized smudge of soot on the man's cheek. He would be, however, the perfect model for Raleigh or Drake.

He leaned on a massive, tempered steel sword, the dull, but obviously, sharp blade unsheathed and menacing in the now glaring light. Its hilt of black leather was worn and frayed as if it were constantly in use for some demonic purpose, slaying dragons or beheading unruly enemy knights. But worse, the man had a menacing aura that was hard to define, but was clearly present to those close to him. Finn could feel it as if it were physical. He almost felt sick. Dara was the first to speak.

"What a surprise!" He stumbled over his words, slightly awestruck of the man, and a touch afraid, it seemed to Finn.

"Yes, my recent ill health has improved, somewhat," the important stranger said. Finn had surmised by now that this must be the unseen and scary Guardian of whom he had heard reference. He did not know how he fitted into the night's strange events, or what relation he might be to him, but he seemed to be the man in charge.

"I see we have found your errant brother." He said to Dara. But he looked straight at Finn.

He snarled; "Tell him this. He has severely displeased me by disobeying, not once, but twice, in a matter of days, a direct instruction not to leave the grounds of this Castle." There was a long pause and the tension in the air physically increased. "Tell him further, that it is for his own safety I make these orders and that people like- that madman- are waiting to crucify him if they can capture him. It is not GOOD ENOUGH!" His voice rose, and he gripped a forklet so tightly that it buckled in his grip. His voice relaxed once more, " ….for him to disobey direct commands."

Dara quickly and sheepishly repeated the rebuke directly to Finn. His entire tone was apologetic, as he would never talk in this way to his brother. Finn had heard every word, but had to hear it all over again, in Dara's feeble intonation of the words.

"I'm right here," he said looking around. " I heard him"

"Finn you know fine and well that he cannot talk to you." Dara hissed through clenched teeth. " But he can make your life difficult, and mine for that matter. You have to watch your step. This banquet is a sham, all for show, but wait until later, when their eyes," and he looked around at the crowd, now ignoring the performance on the stage and merrily eating and drinking again, "…are not here to see."

"Yes, Finn, my dear chap," The Guardian said to a spot somewhere in the middle distance, and unconvincingly graciously. "You shouldn't worry. I am only here to do your bidding, to care for you, to ensure you are safe. My promise to your Parents." And he winked. He looked round and snapped his fingers loudly at two guards, who marched over and escorted him out of the room.

"Enjoy," he said, as he left, smiling.

After that, Finn found it very difficult to enjoy …anything. Here he was, in a strange land with two moons, locked in an enormous, spooky Castle with a psychopathic, ambiguous Guardian to look after him, and all he could rely on was his now enfeebled brother, a shadow of his former self, for safety.

Later that night he tossed and turned in his comfortable soft bed. Sleep should have come easy after such an energetic and different day. After sweeping away gritty gravel from under the mattress, presumably placed there in case some passing princess might try to sleep here, he settled and thought, unable to get the evening's events from his head. In what kind of situation was he? Who was he in this strange land? Why was he here? Had he actually ever been anywhere else? Questions, questions, questions.

Too restless, he reluctantly pulled his body out of the bed and began to walk around the room. An eerie low light followed him wherever he went, providing a personal glow around him, picking up whatever he gazed upon with fovea like precision. He looked at many of the items in the room; a surveyor's theodolite; a sextant; some spoons, bent and twisted to form a humorous sculpture ('A souvenir of Rhyll' it had written in gaudy text on the base); a plaque on the wall featured a green leafy summer scene of a city street from a hillside high above with , yes he could see them quite distinctly; trams and cars…..'Gruß aus Paderborn' it read although the text was old and faded and difficult to read.

There were paintings too, and some he even recognized. Brueghel's '*Hunters in the Snow*' was there. It was a winter scene, with peasant hunters returning to a busy village, with a snowy grey sky into the infinite distance, and detail disappearing as far as the eye could see. He could lose himself in it, look into it forever, and he had done so before, looking for something in the painting that would give him meaning. *Could this be the Homelands*? The land in the painting had always looked unreal and fantastical to him, so why shouldn't it be?

He looked at the bookshelf, full of hardbacks; some were fiction, it appeared, and some weren't. He could see, indistinctly, the red, white and black of a swastika on one book spine and the letters 'A *H. st.ry of W~II*' with an author's name underneath. It was not totally legible. Like a lot of kids his age he had an obsession with this period of 20th century history. It was World War II and the Nazi's atrocities that really grabbed him, and he watched endless hours of documentaries, predominantly focussing on

Hitler, each the same, and each zooming in and providing endless close analysis of the mad and tyrannical Fuehrer. Just how crazy was he? Was it true about his deformity? If he had been killed in WWI how would life be different? If he had been accepted at Art School, or if he was taller, would he have been happier? The programmes trivialised the issue to the 'n'th degree. The reality of what had happened all those years ago was too bizarre for Finn to wholly appreciate, but the strange glamour the media had created about the time was mesmerising. He knew this in the back of his mind, but the holes made all the more exciting. He pulled out the book to look more closely, but on opening it found the text to be completely illegible. It was there in his peripheral vision; he could see written words in a Roman typeface, but when he looked directly at it to read, the words became vague and indistinct.

He pulled out the next book, and it was the same. Every book he looked at had the same illegible writing he could only see from the corner of his eye, with perfect clarity.

"Nothing to read here, then," he thought, musing loudly and puffing noisily and resignedly.

On another bookcase were various older looking books with badly deteriorated covers. These had titles he could read such as ' *Fantastical*

Journeys of Brother Meirion" and "*The Almanac: Twice round the Moons.*" He picked one of these, and found he could read it, if with a bit of difficulty, as it was printed as if by hand on a Gothic press, on thick heavy parchment. The Fantastical Journeys were a collection of memoirs of some…. well, you could only call him a wizard. It wasn't totally clear if he was real or not, but what was here?

There were plates in colour that showed him flying on the back of a raven. Another trudging through the interminable extents of a sandy desert, a green and orange lizard at his feet on a lead, an amulet in his hand, robes aglow in the sun; one where he floated along a river on enormous shoes made of sailing boats, fighting with a horde of cutlass brandishing, eye patch wearing, pirates who were trying to relieve him of a small bag of coins, and more importantly, a map of the Homelands from Croí Dorchadas to the Emerald Ocean. The text seemed to dance merrily, as if asking to be read, so Finn settled on his bed and read for the rest of the night.

The first story was an introduction to Brother Meirion's travels, and recounted how he had ended up in a country where the religious observance meant that every Saint was revered equally. There was a holiday on every Saint's day, and since there were more than 1,123 named Saints, there were more Saints than days, and as no one was allowed to work on the holidays, but had to pray all day; then they were absolutely poor, starving wretches. No industry or trade could flourish, for if you undertook any work on a holiday it was blasphemous and punished by stoning to death. To solve this dilemma a caste of unpoor had been recognised as not worthy of praying to the Saints, and they could provide all the services the Religious Autocracy needed to survive. The country's native population all eventually died off, leaving only a sect of Monks leading the country, and the serfs who waited upon them. They of course eventually got sick of this situation, and rose up in bloody revolution taking control of the country. But then, they were the meritocracy and had to be waited on, and there was no one left to do that, so they all starved to death. Meirion arrived just as the last was dying. When he asked the ex-serf where he was, his last words were that he didn't know the name as no one had ever told him, and then no one knew the name of the land, so Meirion could have been anywhere.

The book also explained to Finn several things, but also highlighted that nothing was as it seemed in the Homelands. Generally, the people, all to a man cat and dog, followed a loose and vaguely tolerant religion, known as Selfism, with no physical leader to answer to, or make up whimsical new rules, and no real observation. You generally lived your life the way that best suited you, without causing harm to anyone else. Nice and simple you would think.

However, in the stories, there was a religious police force, which could accost you at any time, and inquisitorially assess if you were a believer, and what you believed. But since the belief appeared to shift at any given time, your prepared answers might be looked upon as sedition or heresy, and you could find yourself clapped in irons for a few days whilst the religious beliefs themselves morphed into those you did hold. You would then be freed to get on with your life. This had happened to Brother Meirion on several occasions, often due to his inability to decide what his beliefs at that precise moment were or to placate the police with the right ones at the right time. So he often ended up jailed for no reason other than he couldn't get his thoughts straight. He always ended up with a loose moral, his favourite repeatedly being; ' *Life's like that; that's just the way it is....*"

There seemed to be another group who were apart, but they were shown in a line drawing being herded up by the good townsfolk and dispelled from the land, cast adrift on a huge banana shaped boat. Anyway, nothing horrible really ever happened to Brother Meirion. Perhaps these were just fairy tales to help the kids understand how life is.

With dawn's light streaming in the open window, and a light, distant voice whispering his name, the book slipped from Finn's tenuous grip, and fell noisily on the wooden floor, as he finally drifted off to sleep. Strangely, for all his worry, nothing horrible had yet happened to Finn. The Guardian must be too preoccupied with his shiny new prisoner to be bothered about chiding him, he thought, hopefully, in his uneasy sleep.

5 *The Morning*

He awoke suddenly, and the wind was blowing snow in through his open window. Shutters banged against the wall. He shook his head and thought about his dreams, which were elusively disappearing into ether.

What had finished as a pleasant summer night, re-commenced as a cold and miserable winter's morning. He got up, shivering, to close the window that was banging loudly and in danger of breaking the thick glass in the frame. The curtains billowed in the freezing blast but he soon got them shut with a bang and the air in the room became calm once more.

Dressing quickly, he was startled by a knock at the door. On opening it, he squinted in the dawn light and saw a small woman with scarlet hair, cut very short and sharp, and small twinkling eyes visible through enormous bulbous eyeglasses, perched on the end of her extremely long nose.

"Mrs Cooper," she announced curtly. Finn squinted at her as she stuck her foot in the doorway.

"I hear you have been a very naughty young man, and as governess in this Castle, I am here to do something about it. Come this way."

She led him down the stairs through a hallway, and then further down into what could best be described as dungeons. Dank, dark, forbidding dungeons. Finn could hear moaning and groaning, and as he passed one cell, he could hear an incessant babbling. He looked through the tiny window in the door and saw Blaylock sitting on a hard bench, his wild hair flying in all directions, his eyes wide open staring into the distance and gabbling complete nonsense, backwards. There was no sense in what he was saying, and Finn felt that it was very unnerving.

"Get - a – move on," he heard ahead. Mrs Cooper kept moving, scampering on her tiny terrier-like legs, and they soon started climbing again. Finn was becoming a bit worried now, as he had no idea what the next step might bring. It brought him into daylight.

"What a horrible short cut," Said Mrs Cooper. "I do hope it didn't frighten you, too much." Finn heard her add this last bit, under her breath.

They presently came to a tall wooden door marked 'Gymnasium.'

Not so bad, thought Finn, as he entered and stood near the back. It reminded him of an old school hall with climbing bars along the walls and under the thin long windows at the top. Everything looked brown, sepia tinted, as if an old photograph, or someone was smoking a large pipeful of tobacco, just out of view. The early morning sun created swirling patterns in the haze. Various accoutrements relating to sporting deeds and activities such as weightlifting and archery were either scattered across the floor or hanging from the roof. Mrs Cooper pointed to a table, complete with parchment and a quill in the very middle of the room.

"It is as you know, Examination time; Homelish Composition," she said. "I want you to write me a story, in perfect grammar, mark you, and excellent spelling," she ordered sternly. "I want a debate, with a moral at the end. *This House believes one must not disobey direct orders.* Start with that, and think about consequences. Use your head, boy…. You have three hours."

"An exam?" thought Finn with distaste… But it can't be that hard. Three hours, though. Well, if this is what it took to get the harridan off his back then, so be it. However, after only twenty minutes and three pages of writing he smugly piped up, "Finished!" and he attempted to get up from the desk. He found he couldn't. Worse still he could not let go of the quill. His arm was locked onto the desk surface, and his hand had started writing by itself…He tried to stop, but it wouldn't. His hand just continued to write without pause, line after line, getting faster as time progressed. He looked down at the paper, but couldn't even read the writing.

After ten minutes or so had passed, his arm began to tire, and after twenty he was in agony, but his hand still kept moving, the muscles in spasm as they worked hard to keep going. Soon his arm was a blur and to his utter alarm smoke started to spew from the quill tip. Finn's face was now twisted in pain and fear, and he looked imploringly at Mrs Cooper through squinting eyes, but she sat at her desk, knitting intently. "Keep going," she said. "You're doing a fine job. You must be *really* contrite to write quite so much." She said, disingenuously.

The cramps and pain grew worse, and a burning smell soon filled the room, and then, just when he thought he might pass out, his hand slowed and suddenly stopped, with the chilling last line..'… ….*and, Finn McGurrigle, Lord High Protector, shall die*.' The writing had even changed from his own, scrawly handwriting to an artistic Gothic script as if to emphasise the horrifying threat.

Realising, of course, that Cooper had done this to him, he looked angrily in her direction, his eyes narrowing even further, and fury rising in his breast.

"You evil old hag," he shouted, impetuously, and he ran for the door in panic. Mrs Cooper raised her head, madly, and laughed.

"Maybe next time, you will think twice about disobeying The Guardian's wishes," she cackled, and involuntarily winked, the slight tic symbolising her madness. Finn ran from the door and flew right into the ubiquitous Guardian, hitting him squarely in the chest. He winced and watched as Finn bounced off him and then ran past, with a smile of wry satisfaction coming over his face. Finn had automatically said "Sorry," to The Guardian as he ran into him, and almost kicked himself for this stupid reflex response.

Running through the dark dungeons, muttering "Stupid, stupid, stupid," to himself, Finn noticed the oppressive silence, and somehow surmised this had something to do with The Guardian's recent presence. Blaylock's cell door was open, but there was now no prisoner to be seen; only chains on the wall behind where he had sat, babbling, and horrifyingly, a reddened streak of fresh warm blood on the wall. A lone figure stood at the end of the corridor, looking menacing; tall and dark skinned, with a pointed face and sharp white hair and a small whiskery white beard.

"He has been taken from here," said the figure, correctly guessing what was on Finn's mind. "It is not for you to worry about," said the mystery figure. "Grindrod has dealt with him. He will trouble you no more." Finn could tell from the way he spoke that he referred to himself. *He* was Grindrod. Finn didn't even want to imagine what might have happened here, so he just kept running.

6 *A Visit*

Not knowing exactly what to do and feeling a heavy anxiety, let alone aching pain in his arm, he headed for breakfast and was joined by Dara who complained bitterly about the cold. He was hugging own body in the cold emptiness of the banqueting hall, now bare with no revellers, no flags, no bunting, and no band. It seemed a miserly place now; however exotic and exciting it really might have seemed to Finn in this new reality.

"I've just had some sort of punishment," he exclaimed angrily. " It was absolutely awful." He explained what had happened, and Dara tried to reassure him.

"Old Alice is a bit of a monster, isn't she? I've fallen foul of her several times. I can assure you, though, it could get much worse than that. I remember some other boy in the Castle, he was only here a few weeks, and she got hold of him. Well, we never actually saw him again."

And it came back to him, the ginger hair, the wide cheeky grin, the bad behaviour and the theft. That kid had been found wandering the town streets, and no one knew who he might be, or where he had come from. Or if he just went back there. But they did know the last person to take him anywhere was Mrs Cooper. He winced at the thought.

"And look what she did to me," concluded Dara lifting his shirt to reveal a long studded scar on his torso. "This was just for swearing under my breath at The Guardian… she got me across the room with some weird whip with metal attachments. By God, it hurt. What did she look like, by the way? She seems to change every time I meet her. She was a six foot tall blonde when she got me, but you seem to have seen someone different "

"What about the Finn shall die, stuff?" Finn anxiously said, getting the conversation back on track and out of Dara's fantasies.

"She's just being melodramatic; she is a bit…. sort of theatrical; thinks a good sharp shock is good for you, you know? No, no, no. That's not going to happen," he said confidently. "She tried to put a tarantula down my breeches once," he added. "It wasn't real though, just in my head. That threat probably was too…I don't think she would go quite that far." Finn wasn't quite as sure as his brother, though.

A small serving person soon arrived with a plate of hot sizzling sausages and eggs balanced on his head, fat still spitting from them and fizzing. When he removed the tray to place it on the table, Finn saw he wore a hat with a massive flat plate on it to help carry the load. He scurried off, winding back to the kitchens and hobbling on his legs, one of which, Finn noticed in amazement, was fully six inches longer than the other. He was like some sheep, living on a steep mountain slope.

"Anyway, stop thinking about that, it's all over, in the past…We… are going out after this. I think there is someone you need to see," said Dara, conspiratorially. " Even if it is snowing."

As if they were spied upon at all times, which was entirely possible, when they walked out of the front doors their horses were being led up to greet them. Finn rushed over to the fountain first, though, to see the stones that Enid had placed there last night. All he could see at the bottom of the water was a thin film of dust suspended in the, now, icy water. He stuck his hand in and the dust swirled round, heating slightly and glowing again.

It faded quickly as he brought his hand out. It too glowed slightly and he felt a satisfying warmth pass through him. He smiled as he remembered the girl running through the courtyard, but his daydream was spoiled by Percival admonishing them for being outside in the cold. They jumped on their horses and sped off through the Castle gates together, down the cobbled winding streets and out to the outskirts of town, far from the chiding nanny of a man.

They were back in the enchanted forest once more, but this time Dara kept a close eye on his brother. They talked as they travelled, about life in the Castle and the Town, and Finn began to appreciate his high powerful position, the friend he had in this different brother and the great potential that life had for him here. Dara explained, patiently, how the family had been banished from the kingdom and The Guardian had taken over all control. But, that he was only really a figurehead. The Homeland had been some sort of consolation prize for him after he was forced into surrender in a bigger battle waged when the boys were only infants; far in the mists of time as far as they were concerned. The Guardian, it transpired, had at one time been the ruler of an empire so massive it extended beyond all six horizons. All except the Homelands. Dara told Finn how he had explained all this before but Finn somehow kept forgetting.

At that moment, they were startled by a horseman rushing by at speed. He passed by quickly but pulled up to a sudden skidding halt, obviously realising who he had just, accidentally, ignored.

"Great news, sirs, from the Battlefield of Lyre. We have prevailed in the battle. We are advancing on the enemy. They are in retreat. We will be victorious!!! Long live our glorious leader." And with that, he sped off to pass on the glad tidings.

"Surely you know about that?" Dara said looking open mouthed at Finn's confused expression once more…

"The war has been on since, well forever. First we're winning, then they're winning, then it's us again…and so on. We only ever get word from the Front. We are so well protected by the Forest that they can't advance this far. That's the problem with you wandering away, though. Why The Guardian tries to keep you from wandering. If you get beyond the Forest there is no protection until the Front. There are spies and enemies all around and they could just be lurking around the Wastelands. You could get captured, and if they knew who you were it would be all over for us. And, there are tales of weird creatures lurking in the forest, not just wolves or bears, but much worse." Dara looked profound and sad at the thought of this possibility.

"Who are …They?" Finn asked quizzically. "The enemy, I mean…"

"They …are Outsiders. Wastelanders. You've seen one of them already….We get stories about them eating babies for breakfast but they look just like us, so how could they? I mean, how do you cook a whole baby?" He laughed heartily. Finn joined in. He appreciated dark humour, it was often all he had had to keep himself sane in his dark wheelchair bound days; bitter, twisted, dark humour….

They came presently to a small cottage with a thatched roof nestled in a clearing in the forest. The snow was piling up, drifting against its walls. A fire was obviously burning in the grate, judging by the dark smoke exuding from the chimney pot, and it looked cosy, flames flickering through the small thick glass windows, which were made of the glass from some Olde Worlde Shoppe, the kind he'd seen on a Victorian style Christmas card, or in the winding mediaeval streets of old York in England, with a spindle of thick glass at the centre of each pane.

"Why are we here?" Finn asked.

"We're here to see… Mother," Dara replied, triumphantly, having kept this secret for the whole journey even though he was dying to tell. "Just don't let on to that busybody Percival or he might blab."

Finn was completely taken aback at this. This was something out of the blue, even here.

"I thought she was… dead. Back there, she was. Dead. Three years ago." He was confused and troubled, now wondering what was to transpire. Memories of those last three years came flooding back. The crash, the pain, the wheelchair. It was only yesterday after all..

They drew up and dismounted their horses. A woman with long dark hair and a pleasing smiling face looked out from the now open door. It was… his Mum. Finn walked straight up to her and put his arms round her and hugged her as tight as he possibly could, tears streaming from his disturbed eyes.

"I thought I'd never see you again," he said regaining some composure, but still feeling blubbery. " I thought you were dead. But, here you are….How?" There was no answer to this, just, " Things are different now…"

They went inside, and the cottage was as cosy inside as it had looked outside. It looked homely and, whilst darkly lit with a red hue, he could see various nooks and crannies filled with interesting, unusual nick-knacks. Many of these seemed to come from his previous existence from his home, including, he could see, a metallic rocket shaped Alessi Lemon squeezer, a snow globe with a scene of London inside it, and distinctly, a photo of him with Dara in a pewter frame, with the legend "*To my sister Cailin; Always remember that these Boys are not just your Future, Murchadh.**"

"My lovely, handsome, boys," she said as she saw him stare at this strangely out of place item. " Murchadh made it for me, before he ……left us." Finn didn't even stop to think who Murchadh might be and looked around. "Why aren't you at the Castle?" he said, "…. with us I mean."

* pronounced *moor-hah*

She did not answer immediately, but carefully and deliberately poured them a hot steaming fresh tea, and dropped lemon slices slowly into each, serving it with large pieces of a homemade lemon drizzle cake. (*Just the same as she used to* thought Finn with the tears welling again.)

"I can't leave this cottage," she said, "…it's sort of enchanted; it keeps me safe. I can't go to the Castle. If The Guardian knew I was here, he would have me killed. So I can't leave. Murchadh made it safe for me. The Guardian doesn't even think this place exists, now. It means I can see you and your brother, though. I've been watching for some time. I had to send out word with a secret messenger; someone I could trust."

"Enid is a good girl. Her father is a valuable friend of ours. So she is one of us and she is totally trustworthy, someone you can rely upon, any time." (Finn had gasped at the sound of her name; he had seen her not Dara, he heard her name on the breeze, not Dara. He desperately wanted her to be his alone and not to have to share her company with his brother. He was in danger of becoming jealously obsessive about her)

"Dara, only, knows the way here, and he has only just found me. You try and think how you got here and you will find you can't. It is to keep you safe too. If He finds out He will have you interrogated and you might be hurt…. And you, are far too important for that."

Finn was still trying to get to grips with having a Foster parent, and thought that he didn't really seem that bad. A bit stern, a bit of a disciplinarian perhaps; but typical of some oldie he just had different values. That, clearly, was not the case.

"We need you, alive, to get your Father," she announced, unexpectedly. Finn gasped for the second time. "Ah, but, not today…..It's time you left now, the weather is gathering force…..I must rest and wait for him to come back. You must go now." She poured a long glass of a pungent red wine and settled into an armchair, gazing out of the window into the distance as if in a dazed dreamscape.

As they rode off into the gathering storm, heads down and covered by their cloaks, Finn asked Dara why he thought they had to leave, why she wouldn't say any more. It seemed very unfair. He had just found her and she was rejecting him already, it seemed. Dara explained that she needed to rest. She had endured a terrible experience, one that she couldn't even tell him about, let alone explain why she had appeared now. Finn felt slighted. Why had she not sent Enid to him? Why Dara? It was always Dara; he had the life, not him. And even here it was happening. He had the information and Finn was in the dark. He sulked, something he could give master classes in back home.

"It's for your own good," Dara said, anticipating Finn's thoughts. " We need you to be safe…you might not like the fact she came to me, but it means I'm expendable. How do you think that makes me feel?"

Finn had to admit to himself that his was the preferable position in this case. But Dara still knew more than he did. So he stayed silent as they marched back through the steepening streets into the courtyard, where an army of servants ran around chaotically lighting the ancient street lighting system with flickering oil burners, which gave the streets an aura of Christmas in the now blizzard conditions.

7 *Life in Torpor*

Impatience gnawed at Finn's chest. He felt he had to do something to get into action if he was to save the Homeland from a Tyrant, but he couldn't just yet. He didn't know what to do, or how to do it. He had to admit; he didn't really appreciate, yet, what kind of tyranny this misanthropic, bad tempered man could be responsible for. Shouting a lot didn't seem too bad to him. It was just normal, adult behaviour.

As the days of ritual normality spread into one before him he began to get a taste of daily life in the Castle. This was pretty like it had been at home except there seemed to be little education going on. It was the same the end of term at school when he was tutored. Instead of maths and physics, subjects he had excelled in, there was practical help in dealing with warthogs, or alchemical practice, which seemed to him to comprise nothing other than mixing foul smelling liquids together to get an explosion. Good fun though. Often for hours he would stink,, usually of hydrogen sulphide, and he wondered why they just didn't let some eggs go rotten instead of wasting valuable resources on the chemicals. There was great emphasis on horsemanship and various tournament arts.

He even learned how to joust. The practice involved long poles with pillows attached to ensure that no real injury could happen, and he was strung up in a harness connected to a pole which ran along side the jousting rail. When knocked off his horse, he simply swung about in mid air until he was dropped to the ground unceremoniously and embarrassingly.

There was of course sword practice, at which he found himself to be rather good, as though he had been doing it for many years. He thought he was a natural, and boasted to Dara about his apparent instinctive prowess. Dara told him how he hadn't looked so good at last year's tournament, when he was roundly defeated by a one legged troll.

"The Guardian was utterly affronted by your useless attempts," he explained, " and made you practice swordsmanship for three hours every day. You soon improved."

Finn could obviously remember nothing of this, but at least the boredom of the practice had gone with his memory, and he had at least the benefit.

"Cool," he thought to himself, thinking gleefully of how this would all be impossible in his wheelchair.

"There's a return match this year," Dara informed him, smirking, at which Finn gulped visibly, for practice was one thing but facing an armed experienced adversary was completely different.

"When's this then?" Finn said, hoping he might have returned to the real world and out of this dream life before then.

"Two weeks from now, I think," and Dara changed the subject, pointing over at a young man pacing in front of the Castle walls.

"That's Cedric; he'll be looking for his brother, Godric, I bet. Lets go and talk to him."

Finn looked quizzically, and in amazement watched the man pace thoughtfully up to the walls and disappear, before they could get near him.

Dara continued, knowledgeably, and in a gossipy manner.

"Cedric and his brother are both alchemists. They are supposed to have stumbled upon a potion months ago that enabled them to walk through walls. Thinking it would be invaluable for The Guardian, they were trying to perfect it. Took to testing it on them selves. Godric walked through the wall, just about there, a couple of weeks ago, and he hasn't been seen since. Cedric has been distraught. Percival told me all about it. Seems it was his entire fault. He misread the ingredients and made up a potion at only half the concentration it should have been…Godric took it, walked through the wall, and it wore off half way through. And there he is, buried alive. Of course Cedric can't tell if he simply suffocated, or if the potion keeps him alive or what, so he is trying to find him. But where do you start? Have to be careful what you put in your mouth, don't you think?"

The two weeks passed interminably slowly, with a succession of meals and classes, and classes and even bigger, elaborate meals, and occasional wandering in the confines of the town; just the two of them. Nothing really happened, and even worse, the dullness of life without computer equipment soon became unbearable to Finn.

On one occasion, though, they did happen to bump into Enid, which brightened Finn's day enormously. She still said nothing, but her body language said enough for all the words in the worlds. Finn stammered as he spoke to her, but at least he said something, he hopefully thought.

"Why doesn't she ever speak?" Finn asked Dara later, convinced she just wouldn't speak to him.

"She doesn't need to," he explained. "If you listened hard enough, you can hear her; well more precisely, *you* can hear her, but no one else. Mother said there was some stupid prophecy in some ancient book she has. Apparently, a great leader will arrive from a vague world outside and save the Homelands, and he will take as his bride and queen an Ice Maiden. She can only communicate with this man. The book has some fantastic artwork, you know," he added.

"So Mother told me that she thinks that Enid is somehow the Ice Maiden, and well, she thinks the sun shines out of your backside, so to her, you are the great leader. And you seem to be from somewhere else, all the time! I just don't understand you sometimes."

"Anyway, she has great hopes for a big wedding in a free land, with doves and flags and a train of carriages all the way through the town. She told me not to tell you that bit, because you either are or you aren't, and the pressure to perform won't help you one bit. Anyway, if the prophesy is true, Dad's going to do the job and he's already married to Mother, so, how does that all work? It's religious mumbo jumbo as far as I'm concerned."

Yet again, Finn was dumbstruck.

"A prophecy; about me?" he thought, "..And Enid and, erm, fighting." The pressure mounted immediately. Though, of course, Dara might have some nefarious and ulterior motive, recounting a story he couldn't possibly confirm. Anyway, he had plenty of time to mull it over as the tournament preparations progressed.

"She seems to tell you an awful lot," Finn finally commented, with suspicion.

The courtyard was being transformed into an arena for the sport, and as they arrived, hordes of tradesmen and carpenters were busy at work. Scattered around the ground were gigantic flagpoles with enormous flags attached, waiting patiently to be hoisted into position. Finn marvelled at the height of tree that would be needed to be felled to produce even one of these magnificent decorations.

They were on foot now. Passing by the skeleton of a grandstand, Finn noted the workmen high above him, all busy hammering and sawing and tying and weaving. He was too busy looking at the highest workers to notice anything else. He could see very little clearly as the sun was blinding him.

An iron mallet fell innocently from a hand directly above him and dropped noiselessly towards him, heading directly for his head, unprotected and fragile. A weak call was made, which only those high up in the scaffold could hear. At the last minute, still blinded and looking up, he stumbled over a timber joist, and the hammer fell dangerously close by his ear landing at his side. He jumped, startled by the enormous potentially fatal weight, which had just missed him by inches. When he remembered to breathe he asked Dara if he had seen anything, but Dara just said, "It must be an accident, there are so many incompetents up there, who knows?"

There was a bright flash, the origins of which were unidentifiable, and next thing a carpenter, tools and all, was falling through the air, arms flailing, screaming in pain and exclaiming his regrets for some unknown deed. He hit the ground with a thud and the dust around him rose, formed a cloud then settled. No one came to his aid, and his lifeless body lay where it had landed, faint wisps of smoke leaking from the folds of his loose sackcloth, his head twisted on the ground, drooling.

Finn and Dara had heard the scream, and turned to see the mass hit the ground, and surmised instantly together that this was the unfortunate who had accidentally dropped a hammer, having suffered some sort of seizure, or sudden illness. But they knew no way to help and assumed his workmates would come to his aid. Before they could, however, an armed guard appeared from the Castle, jogged over and picked him up. He was never seen again.

The next few days passed easily with no further incidents. Finn's life was settling into a routine of meals and lounging around watching the preparations for the tournament. No more hammers or falling people.

The morning of the tournament arrived and the sun shone down from early morning in a cloudless azure blue sky. The prospects were good. Following a hearty breakfast, Finn and Dara selected their best and most fashionable clothing. As Crown Princes this tended to be whatever they decided on the day. Who was going to argue with them? The Guardian had been noticeably absent for a few days so life was simple. No menace. But to their chagrin, this morning he appeared again, striding into Finn's room with Dara in tow to translate. He seemed in a good exulted mood. It was showtime, and this was his show.

He led them in procession to the arena where they took their prominent seats in the royal box, directly in front of the action. After some interminable time The Guardian stood, and in a raised powerful voice announced to the crowd that the tournament was to begin. A thousand orange doves were released from a box behind them. This was spectacular, but the guano festival also started there. Finn looked at the goo dropped from the birds on his newest clothes in disgust. He looked at The Guardian. His blackest robes were smattered with white and orange, and he snarled at the birds, and raising his sword high above his head a bolt of blue white piercing light emanated from the tip and struck a single dove in mid flight. It was fried instantly and fell to the centre of the arena to the massed guffaws of the audience. He seemed satisfied with this minor revenge, and sat down, after a small bow to the crowd. Finn was awestruck at the power of the sword, and stood open-mouthed gaping at it. The Guardian noted this and smiled smugly at him. Finn thought he was surely planning to use this on him.

The entertainment began in earnest, with a parade of captured prisoners from the Battlefield. To make their humiliation complete the raggle-taggle group was made to drop their breeches in the centre of the arena, and a select group of children, the families of fallen soldiers, was allowed to whack them broadsword over the buttocks. As they were marched off another sector of the audience, obviously primed, pelted them with specially rotted fruits. A group of disgruntled guards also ended up stinking, but could not really protest. They joined in the carnival atmosphere, laughing joyously.

Next up came a parade of the walking wounded, smiling and waving flags and they were marched across the arena to cheers and hoots from the crowd. A platform was raised in the centre and two young dazzling blond men appeared, strong jawed and clean-cut, and stepped onto the platform. They made a jingoistic and patriotic speech describing their exciting adventures on the battlefield, the enemy they had massacred, and the ease of life in the Homeland Armed Force. The army poster boys then wandered round the arena throwing shillings into the cheering crowd who ate it up in a frenzy of patriotism. To a man they would have marched on the enemy that instant; that was of course after the day's entertainment and beer and grub. Tomorrow would be soon enough, after the hangover.

The entertainment continued in earnest with the Jesters. Finn recognised them as the two he had first met at the Banquet Hall. They were very entertaining and provided a counterpoint to the show trial atmosphere of the last hour, the famous Del Fuego Brothers, Ruari & Robino, known countrywide as the Homeland's finest entertainers, made light of The Guardian in a parody of his famous fiery temper. Only today would they have his indulgence to escape with their lives for such utter disrespect. They walked a dangerous line, closely mimicking the foibles of the tyrant. In one particularly brilliant, observational, and highly satirical, note they howled at the crowd together like wolves, pining for the moons.

One day, Finn knew, they would go too far and The Guardian would have them dispatched without a second thought, and replace them with a troupe of midgets, for which he seemed to show a particular affection. He kept one or two as though they were pets, and they performed tricks to amuse him in dull moments.

The tournament turned out pretty much as Finn had expected. There was jousting, wrestling, men battling with all manner of deadly metallic weapons trying to knock each other's blocks off. Strangely though this part was duller than he expected it might be.

But then it was his turn to joust and the boredom turned to anxiety. He was led away and fitted out in his new armour, procured specially for the day. It seemed to weigh a ton. It was the full works, Chain mail underneath, and metal covering all over from breastplate to thigh coverings and greaves (for the lower leg), and finally on his feet spiked shoes known as sabatons. He picked up each of these phrases as the Squires threw the armour to each other, in dressing him. He felt as though he were an action figure brought to life, the plaything of these underlings.

He could hardly walk. The armour was all in the most spectacular indigo, glinting in the sun with a spectrum of all the other colours.. Finally his helmet was placed on his head. The same bluish steel, it was topped with a flamboyant bright pink feather three feet high, as though just plucked from a flamingo that minute. He soon felt incredibly self-conscious, waddling uncomfortably towards the horse paddock.

His horse was brought out, and he mounted. His horse was by far the tallest most magnificent beast on the field, and this made him feel confident. It too was fitted with the finest new armour, with a crinet, covering the neck area, a peytral shining with spectral colours on his chest, and most magnificently a piece of head protection known as a shaffron. He had innocently asked if the armour had a name and got the full lecture…This metal covering was translucent blue, shimmering in the sun and had holes for its eyes and finally a single horn making it appear as a unicorn.

His squire was shouting up at him giving him tips and advice on the best way to tackle Bedevere, his combatant. Then, the time came. Silence reigned, apart from the snorting of his horse Erik, and soon the handkerchief dropped and he had to fly. Racing along the fence, his lance seemed too heavy for him to lift but he soon got the centre of gravity right and balanced it between his hip and his right elbow. He sat it finally on the lance rest sticking out from the breast plate. Bedevere bore down on him and seemed incredibly terrifying in his black armour and ultra tall armoured helmet with his trademark symbol on the front. Three waves in a circle. He was so arrogant he also carried his flag aloft too. It was black and white bands, and fluttered wildly in the wind.

Then they clashed. In a slow motion split second, Finn hit Bedevere squarely on the breastplate with the tip of his lance. He expected to feel the sudden impact on his chest and to be knocked flying from his horse, or to be knocked from his mount by the sheer force of Bedevere's massive bulk. But, to his surprise and horror, the tip of the pole sliced through Bedevere as though he were butter; as though he simply did not exist.

The knight's torso slid down the pole towards Finn who was now aghast at what he had done and felt sickened and nauseous. All around were cheering and laughing and then he realised that there was no mass in the target he had struck, it was an empty void, a suit of armour with no substance, and as Finn dropped the lance it fell to the ground with a loud clanking sound and the body crumpled, the helmet fell off, and the formless void within burst open and more doves flew out. Finn heaved a sigh of relief, and in the tents ahead the squires laughed loudly and pointed at Bedevere, massive and blubbery in his undergarments dancing foolishly, grinning and gesturing at the dim Prince, duped by his servants. Tradition, it became apparent, suddenly. Hence the gaudy armour…Finn sighed at the realisation that he was the fool, today.

Finn rode back to the tents and dismounted, still shaking. He walked slowly back to his seat, but found he couldn't concentrate on the events in front of him. He should have been concentrating for as he discussed the joust with Dara at the back of the box, a group of jesters appeared in the front, juggling badly, making pratfalls, and squabbling with each other. As they arrived directly in front of the box, one drew out a pineapple from under his costume and lobbed it directly into the box, where it landed with a resonant and heavy thud at the feet of The Guardian. He looked down for an instant, surprised. And saw it was smoking. Soon, a thick cloud of acrid smoke billowed from the fruit and filled the box. All were coughing and spluttering but The Guardian simply and coolly picked up the device and, laughing, threw it back into the midst of the clowns. They split up and ran in different directions, but the militia were soon on the spot picking each one off as they tried to escape.

The Guardian had one directly in his sights and he raised and then pointed his sword at the man. He gazed down its length as if taking aim, one eye closed. A humming buzzing light emanated from the tip, and he spun it once round his head as if it were a Venezuelan Bola. With a final flick of his wrist, the energy flew at the fleeing man and hit him squarely between the shoulders bursting in a blue light and spreading over his back. The man literally exploded in front of their eyes, to the gasps and horror of the crowd. The awe, though, was soon replaced by rapturous applause as the crowd cheered and raised their hats and clapped up at the Royal Box. As if it were part of the show. Normality had returned. The Guardian gave a good natured nod at the crowd and grimacing sat down to enjoy the continuing spectacle.

The mess was soon swept away and the tournament resumed as though nothing had happened; as though this was a regular occurrence, or as though this event happened every year for the crowd's delectation.

Finn was feeling thoroughly sick now, and whispered to Dara. They both stood up and left, much to the obvious disgust of The Guardian, who presumably felt they were feeble.

They made their way back to the Castle, to ruminate over the day's events. Finn found he had no appetite at that night's banquet, but he had to attend anyway in his ceremonial capacity, and smile at the local dignitaries who had come to display their ostentation. The music and the wine would soon wash away the horror he had felt too much that afternoon, and before long he was in oblivious disconnection to this horrible frightening world, grinning inanely at the jesters and the spinning party goers arranged in front of him.

Later, as he slept, he was visited by disquieting dreams. He was in the air swooping low over his home town, back in the 21st Century. The birds were singing merrily in the trees, and around him life was progressing as normal, but something was amiss. He soon found out what it was; what was churning in his mind.

There was his little house with its curtains closed to the daylight. Grim faces were all around and there was Dara, distraught, leading his Dad, bent and broken to a black car. Silent morning dressed men nodded at them, holding the door of the car to speed them on their way. Behind he soon became aware of the menacing long hearse.

"Where am I?" He thought, but dismissed this thought, then confidently sure this was the scene from three years ago he had missed in the Hospital. But then a terrifying sight, he had never thought he would see was in front of him. The wreath was garish, and childish in away he thought, looking from this distance, but said it all in four utterly clear, blue letters;

"FINN"

8 *The Camera Obscura*

The next day he awoke, sweating, to the sun streaming through his window once more. The rain of the previous evening was gone and it was the start of what should be a perfect summer's day. Once he had stopped feeling ill, Finn had determined that today he would try to find out what had happened to his Father. His dream troubled him, for he felt there could be no way back now, and he knew his future was here. Glumly he headed down the stairs. Breakfast, today, was held in a small room and comprised a weird potato cake fried lightly and served with sugary syrup and orange coloured, banana-shaped fruits. He still had no appetite, but since this was largely self-inflicted he forced himself to eat. He ruminated on his dream throughout, alone in this dank room.

As he left the breakfast room he was aware of a group of small scurrying figures running through the corridors.

"Orphans," Percival said, appearing smoothly from the shade of an alcove. He seemed to glide out on wheels again. " We just cannot catch them, but then they do such little harm, the poor mites," he said in a patronising, sneering voice.

The ragged, undernourished, kids infested the tower, living the life of sewer rats, ducking in and out of the shadows, running through the myriad corridors of the Castle looking for any sustenance they could, each more aware of the dark secrets of this frightening place than Finn could possibly imagine. But he was becoming more aware with every hour and every person he met that not all was right in this place. The Guardian for one; the mysterious and dangerous Foster Parent he could not have wanted in a thousand years with his enigmatic, powerful past, his new simmering resentment and his potent danger to Finn. How could he avoid displeasing this tyrant?

Dara suggested a good, but unexciting idea. Up in the Observatory there was a mad scientist, a soothsayer who ran the Observatory and who, for a few silver coins, would let them have access, as long as they did not touch anything of course, and they could look out into the Wasteland through the massive, powerful telescope.

When they got into the observatory, which occupied the topmost portion of the green dome, which Finn had noticed on his way here, they were ushered in by a small, wild haired man with a stoop and a gnarled walking stick.

"Come in, come in, we have few visitors here. No one is interested in my work you know."

"Oh we are!!! Please tell us all about the stratosphere, Dr Spangler," Dara said, passing him, surreptitiously, a small bag of coins.

"Oh, good…I see you are very, very interested," he said delightedly looking into the bag and slipping it into a small purse dangling from his belt. "Before we look through the telescope, might I suggest the Camera Obscura?"

"Yeah, that'll do for starters," Dara said, leading the way to a winding set of steps up to a buckled, mahogany coloured doorway. This led to a small, darkened room, right atop the dome. In the middle of the room was a round table painted white, with ropes and cables dangling above it. High above it, in the roof space, was a cylinder with a strange arrangement of mirrors

"Let me see, let me see," the old man said…. and he started to pull on the strings.

As if by magic, which Spangler, of course, pretended it was and as though these were three year olds he talked to, an image of the courtyard in real time appeared on the table. It was upside down. The boys humoured him and gave each other knowing eye-rolling glances in the darkness behind his back, gagging and trying not to burst into raucous laughter. They taunted each other with their eyes, defying each other to make a noise.

"Come, come round here," the old man ordered. "I can fix it!"

They followed round and the image was now the right way to be viewed. They obligingly 'ooohed,' at the image to keep the old man happy. He was so old that anyone under fifty probably seemed to be a small child to him, so these teenagers were babies as far as he was concerned.

The scene in front of them was a busy street scene. Crowds moved around aimlessly. The boys spotted three colourfully dressed figures sporting large hats, walking in single file with a hand on each other's shoulders. The lead one rang a bell to clear the path ahead.

"The Three Fools!" shouted Dara " I haven't seen them in weeks." Looking around they saw a contingent of the armed guard, apparently on some free time, wandering the streets. There was a woman with a kite, which kept lifting her off the ground, and several ragged kids ran about, playing with wheeled toys. A goat ran across the screen and ran headlong into one of the Fools who fell into a pile of steaming manure at the roadside.

The crowd laughed and pointed as he picked himself up and joined the back of the queue. A passer by joined in with them and marched along the street dancing. The Fools remained oblivious. A scrawny, flighty, ragged figure with straggly hair and a wispy beard passed by them, and bumped,

Finn thought deliberately, into one of the crowd, laughing at the sight. Finn pointed to him and Dara exclaimed, "Look, that's Dribble! Percival says he's a master criminal, but he looks more like a pickpocket if you ask me. Still, he's never been caught red handed, so who can tell? He'll get his come-uppance one day and The Guardian won't be subtle about it!"

Dribble melted into the crowd, not to be seen again, but the voyeur he had bumped could be seen angrily looking for his money purse, which had been tied to his belt. His curses could be made out even in the silence. "Was I right, or was I right?" said Dara.

They saw the guards again, looking into a public house and gesturing. They were laughing at some unheard joke. Next, there was a man pushing a barrow filled with exotic green and yellow fruits, and multicoloured birds which they could see squawking silently. Whilst mildly entertaining, it was a bit dull compared to the potential exhilaration of looking through the huge exciting telescope downstairs. Just then, though, they noticed in unison something out of the ordinary that raised their interest. The guards were standing outside a shop and appeared to be shouting and gesturing angrily at someone unseen inside the door.

Next they drew out missiles; rocks or something from within their tunics, and threw them right at the door and the windows of the shop.

People inside the shop ran out to the door, and gesticulated, but then cowered inside, again. Two of the guards pushed their way into the now closing doorway and grabbed one of the people inside, dragging him out of the shop. At first they thought it was a woman, and they couldn't believe their eyes at the violent attack. Then they realised it was a man. Whilst it didn't excuse the violence, it seemed less unusual or unpredictable. The man, who wore a long lime green dress, hence the confusion, was thrown violently into the street whereupon the rest of the guards set upon him, hitting and kicking him. The two intruders pushed the other occupant into the street too, and next thing the building was ablaze, black, putrid smoke billowing from the broken panes and the doorway. The guards laughed and carried on hitting the people. A few townspeople shouted at the guards, but they were scared off as one of them made towards them with his sword brandished. Soon he was back at the unfortunates on the roadway, who, whilst still alive, must have been within a hair's breadth of their lives by now. Then, a cart drew up, the victims were piled on and the cart headed to the Castle gates.

Shocked and totally stunned by what they had witnessed, the two brothers stood awestruck and dumb. What was this about? What could these people have done? They looked back at the table and saw a few townsfolk braving the flames to run into the shop. Some came out gleefully carrying away prized possessions, but one came out with a baby in his arms and handed it to a woman. He raised his fist at the guards and shouted something. They looked back and to a man laughed at him. One got off the cart and lunged at the man with a sword. It only grazed him but he fell to his knees in terror. The guard walked off smiling, and soon the scene was one of normality apart from the burning building and the air of an atrocity having happened in this sleepy town.

Finn and Dara ran from the room, down the spiralling stairs and tried to find out what was happening. They gabbled to Percival who told them they must have imagined it, for nothing quite so horrific had ever been known to happen in this town, and the Armed Guard were here to protect the townsfolk, not attack them. And off he wheeled.

"The dungeons, I know where they are," said Finn. " Lets get down there and see what's going on." But the door was barred. That didn't stop the noise getting through, though, and the horrifying screams could be heard until the early afternoon when they abruptly stopped.

Finn decided there was nothing they could do, so they both headed out of the Castle to look at the location of the perpetrated horror. When they got to the site, the strangest thing was the normality. They couldn't really be sure this was the right location, but looking around they realised it was. However, there was no burnt out shell of a building, no panicking crowd, no hostility, and more to the point the shop was open to custom, selling baked goods with a full display of tarts and cakes in the bay windows, unbroken and whole. A smiling, cheery, rotund face welcomed them in as they entered the bakery and recognising them instantly proffered free samples.

"We don't see you lads down here often," the red face said. " What a pleasure. Do tell The Guardian that we make the best speciality cakes in the town and we can supply any number…"

Surprised, they left, walking quietly into the sunny daylight shaking their heads in disbelief.

"I am absolutely, one hundred percent sure that was real," said Finn. "What about those poor people? What's happened to them?"

"Maybe it was somewhere else; the cakes were good, don't you think?" suggested Dara, unassertively, and to tell the truth, unhelpfully, for they both knew instinctively that something here was awfully wrong.

They looked at each other in blank amazement and turned to go back to the Castle. Neither spoke on the way back, but each knew the other was going over the events in their head.

Finally, Finn broke the silence.

"Do you think The Guardian knows about this happening? I mean, his armed guard going into places and beating up the occupants, on what appears to be a whim. I've seen this sort of thing on the news before,"

Dara looked blankly at him, wondering what he meant by seen, and news.

"It's what happens in dictatorships everywhere, you know, like Hitler and the Nazis, or Cambodia, or North Korea .....well, I suppose you don't know. And The Guardian seems loopy enough to me to do almost anything. What could he want with a shopkeeper, though? "

"So who is Hilter?" asked Dara.

"Hitler," Finn corrected him. "Oh, sorry, I forgot. You wouldn't know anything about him. He was a crackpot German Dictator who tried to take over a Continent and caused a massive War, back where I'm from. Systematically murdered millions ......wait a minute, those weird clothes. That shopkeeper wasn't part of some sect was he? Y'know, a religion? That's the sort of thing the Nazis did to people, at the start. Smashed up their property, took it over and ...." his voice trailed off for a second. ".... Well, some really serious other stuff. They tried to annihilate an entire race. That sort of stuff isn't going on here is it?"

Dara looked sheepish and tried not to look at Finn as though hiding some innocent secret.

"I've heard some stories" he said, " but that's the first thing like that I've ever seen. It was a bit of a laugh before. You would go and shout names at them, for wearing women's clothing, you know. Some kids threw mud at them. They can't fight back, they're absolute pacifists. They just let you walk all over them." He looked ashamed of his secret. "You didn't know, and anyway, I know you wouldn't have joined in."

9 Decision Time

Trudging heavily back into the Castle Finn sought out Percival. He wanted to speak to The Guardian and see what he might know about the events. He was amazed at his sudden change. A new assertiveness. It was as if some distant, long forgotten training had kicked into place. He felt he had the absolute right to know what was going on, even if it meant confronting the tyrant potentially perpetrating it. He was the heir to a kingdom after all, so he had the right to know. Dara held back and sloped off to his rooms. Finn, almost arrogantly and as though he owned it, which of course he did, strode around the empty hall seeking his new foe; tense and nervous, but no longer afraid of what he might find. Enervated and alive again, he felt the simple power of his legs transporting him in a way he had never felt before.

"Good to see you're still here, Finn," The Guardian said to Percival as they found him in his chamber looking over some papers, presumably tax figures or armed strategy. Finn could not tell for the script was wholly alien to him. Percival passed on the information. The Guardian signalled for him to leave. Alone, Finn moved to a hard wooden bench under some stairs that led, apparently, to nowhere, two flights up in the hall. He felt secure though, surrounded on all sides in this place.

"Wait here," The Guardian said, and he proceeded to set up an elaborate system of mirrors…."This will help. The spell that fool Murchadh put on me before I dispatched him, might work in some ways, but he was no lawyer." The Guardian said menacingly. " He didn't look at the fine print closely enough before setting it off."

"Ahh now, that's much better isn't it. Now we can talk to each other. Man to man, I suppose we have to say now. Look at you. Haven't you changed?" He said this patronizingly as he sat down in a comfortable chair and looked at Finn through the mirrors.

"Yes; nothing to say I can't communicate effectively with a reflection, provided it's not actually you. You are in luck, though, that I can't quite work out how to… harm you in any way." And he laughed, raucously. "Only joking, young Finn…."

"Yeah, sure," thought Finn, now convinced he already knew the answers to his un-posed questions. He explained clearly and in simple terms the events he had just witnessed.

"I feel you are worried that this is part of a bigger picture, Finn?"

Finn involuntarily nodded, giving himself away.

"I understand you invoked the name, Hitler? We have our sources you know, and you can rest assured I am no….Hitler."

Finn was confused that he both knew about the conversation and about that name.

"All sorts of information gets to us, too, you know. My father, for instance was there, in a place named Berlin. Well, it must have been what you would refer to as 1945, whatever that means. He was very young, and the carnage, the death, the destruction, affected him greatly. Idealism."

"Not always good for the soul!" he said finally, gauging Finn's reaction to this titbit of information, simply thrown in as an opener, this strange acknowledgement of another world, his world.

Taken aback by this, Finn's mind raced but he could not put his thoughts together coherently. "What was his motive?" Finn thought, as the menacing figure smiled at him.

"He arrived there by accident of course. Willed himself somewhere... different.... to escape the banality of this place. And it worked. He wanted adventure and he got it. Him and that fool Murchadh messing about with rune stones and stupid spells, I gather. He was lucky to get back home, of course. In a situation such as that anything could have happened. If it had gone wrong, I might not even have existed, imagine that? He made it his duty to make me completely aware of the existence of this other world. I mean, I thought they were like fairy tales to start with, the way he told them too me, at bedtime."

"The technology for instance; things that these simpletons here can only dream about. We have our methods here, though, that would outwit the minds of even the greatest scientists in the Other Place. Simple magic, or perhaps a greater technology? Who could possibly tell the difference?"

"Anyway, when you said that name, I knew instantly you had been there too. You must tell me what it's like some time. I gather our man lost that war."

"Back to the matter in hand, though. I suggest you forget what you think you have seen. I think you can also rest assured that this is of no consequence to you. A matter of unpaid tax, I believe. That man has defrauded you and I have seen fit to punish him for his…. misdemeanour. It may have looked bad, but he is safe; unharmed practically. A few nights in a cell, and he'll be back on his feet, and in business again."

"But what about the fire, the new shop?" Finn interjected, not believing a word.

"Yes, unfortunate. That fool has lost his shop. Confiscated to pay his dues. He will have to start again from scratch. We have many more deserving townsfolk, don't you think?"

"What about the others, in the dungeons, I mean, and the screaming?"

"Ah yes, plotters, seditionists. How many can there be? And all a danger to *you*, you know."

"How can they be a danger to me?" He asked. "They don't even know I exist."

Finn sat on the cold floor under a stairwell and glared out defiantly knowing the truth was different. The Guardian now sat with his head balanced on his thumbs, his hands together over his mouth as though in prayer. In the silence, water dripped from overhead and splashed noisily onto the stone floor, into a green algae puddle. Given enough time a stalagmite would form here.

Staring intently at this, Finn's mind wandered from the imminent threatening present to the distant future, where this Castle was in ruins, and this basement was being discovered by adventurous archaeologists; lights on their helmets and anticipation on their breath. They could not know the horrors of this chamber; the deaths and the torture that must have taken place here. Finn was only vaguely aware of the truth here and it was too much for his young mind to handle. He trembled.

The Guardian gazed deeply into the mirror. Finn could see him clearly, and it was obvious The Guardian could see him cowered under the stairs.

"Finn, you must realize that our fates are bound together. This stone," He raised the sparkling, indigo coloured gemstone on a chain round his neck, " ..is the source of all power in the Homeland."

"Someone else, some other person, also appears to have enough of this beautiful stone to enable the power they gain from it to influence into this kingdom, and to protect you. As Guardian, I have absolute control of the mines. This …person," There was a definite distaste in his tone, "is a thief and shall be hunted down and destroyed. When I have their share of the Blue Moonstone, then you will no longer be protected by it. No one will in fact, and my reign of terror can begin in earnest. I will bring darkness down on this land and destroy my enemies with a vengeance more frightening than you with your puny imagination, can think of. Your Hitler will be like a puppy dog compared to the destruction I can wreak with…well, perhaps I've said too much."

"This gives you a stark choice. Give up the fight and join me, or die. But, the trouble is your stupid principles…and the fact, of course, you simply do not trust me. You cannot join me…so die it is, Finn, only, obviously not today…."

"I have tried to create a home for you here. Even though I was under constant pressure, and held in this Castle, this prison, against my will, by an even higher power.........you and that wretched brother just do not appreciate what you have and can have here."

"Your Mother and Father did not appreciate the power here. What could be achieved in this Land. They fled like lemmings when I attacked, leaving you here to rot, it seems. When I walked, no... strode into this Castle, you were sleeping in your rooms as if they had just gone out for a ride on a summer's day. Your brother was a toddler and he cried to the wind. You bit my arm when I first picked you up." He laughed as if this were a fond memory of a child of his own.

"You had teeth like a lion's. They couldn't have been real, though, but I still have the scar. When I tried to talk to you the pain came. Excruciating pain. I soon learned to talk indirectly and the pain simply went away."

"I sent out hounds and an army to find your Parents, the most vicious ones I could find and I had to pay heavily. They did not need to look far. A cottage in the clearing; how quaint and romantic. There they were, side by side, lying in a bed of down on that fateful morning."

"When I was done with them though, they wished they had stayed here for the merciful release of a swift death. I left them down here in the capable hands of Grindrod. He tells me they screamed your name three times in unison as they died. A bit too melodramatic for my tastes, but what can you expect?"

Finn smiled to himself, smug in the knowledge that his parents were not dead, and that his mother now lived on, in the same cottage in the clearing. But how come The Guardian wasn't aware of this or the cottage or everything? Grindrod cannot be as good at his job as he thought, but he must be incredibly brave or incredibly stupid to lie to The Guardian. Finn knew his father was far away plotting his return, planning to return to the Castle and take back his birthright. But where was he now?

The Guardian continued, "Look, Finn, your destiny would be the same; you are the future ruler of this place, whatever happens. I am merely a caretaker. And I am getting older. Do you know I lost my wife, Dagmar, long ago, in the wars? She was beautiful, fine, but not a fighter. Not suited to these times. One day she was there, the next she wasn't. I still, to this day, don't know what happened to her, but I have my suspicions, and your family figure pretty highly in them. We all have our troubles, Finn."

"I try to bring order out of chaos, peace out of war and harmony out of discord, and what thanks do I get. Plotters, dissidents, rebels, backwoods fighters, whisperers, and gossipmongers; all betraying me and my vision. Do you think it is easy ruling with an iron fist, ensuring your orders are followed, that your lieutenants are loyal and not plotting your overthrow behind your vulnerable back?"

"Did you know that someone somewhere has even cursed me. Every time the twin moons are at full I am stricken down with a fever, a pain, a pounding headache, which will not let me rest. I howl to the moons to get it to stop, to go away."

"I scream at the moon to die sometimes. It's that bad. And I know it will return month after month, year after year, decade upon decade. Does anyone feel sorrow for me? No."

"What I need is someone I can trust; a son of my own to follow me, but that cannot be, so instead I have ....you. But you will not follow will you? You are arrogant and independent and despise and distrust me. What basis is that for a father son relationship?"

"Pretty normal for a teenager," thought Finn, amused now by the openness of the tyrant. "He does have a human side it seems..."

This was no time to become sentimental about a raving paranoiac psychopath, bent on not only his ultimate destruction, but everyone's thought Finn and he launched himself from the stairwell and across the room, taking his chances to escape. The Guardian lunged out at him as he passed, but as he touched him a pain crossed his forehead and he winced in agony stopping short of grabbing Finn's tails. He careered out the door and ran up the stone steps to freedom.

"Guards!...Guards!....release the bats!" Finn could hear The Guardian shouting in the distance. The utter ridiculousness of this phrase was all Finn could think about as he ran. Soon he was in the open air and running across the Castle courtyard to the gates. His horse was being readied by a knave, Erickson: son of Erick, as if he had known Finn would be coming right that moment. Finn leaped on to the horses back, kicked his heels, and flew out of the grounds at full speed.

He looked over his shoulder to the Castle and saw a vague black cloud swarming from a void below the tallest tower.

"So, he wasn't saying that for a laugh then," thought Finn as he became aware that the swarm was a cloud of millions of bats; so many he could actually hear them squealing as they bore down on him. After a minute or so the first of them caught up with him and he was soon enveloped in the black writhing cloud. He was having difficulty breathing, for they seemed to sit on his face and grab at his clothes and hair and bite him ferociously with tiny gnawing teeth. Unable to see, he headed onwards, trusting his horse to be able to outrun the swarm, but not sure that he would survive. The squealing noise became intolerable and the biting and their feathery grip overcame him and he felt himself drifting as though being lifted from his saddle and taken by flight.

From nowhere, a wind brewed up and became violent, noisy and stunning. The flimsy bodies of the individual bats was no match for this natural wonder and they were blown each and every way, detaching from him and flying off into the distance, smashing against buildings and rocks, and soon the streets were littered by the twitching, warm corpses of tiny bats, each pitiful in its private demise; its tragedy, its grim, communal, death. Finn and his horse seemed to be immune to the wind, which disappeared as quickly as it had been conjured up, for that is how it seemed. Townsfolk looked on in dread and amazement as the swirling whirl wind dissolved into nothingness. All to a man and woman stood in awe looking in Finn's direction.

All, but a tall loner in a cloak, who ran from the scene, on springheeled boots. A blue aura escaped from under his cloak as it billowed in the breeze. Finn's saviour was escaping from the scene. Who was this? How was he at the right place at exactly the right time to save him? How do I catch him? Thought Finn. He took up pursuit.

He was the wind now and he rode, kicking up a hurricane through the streets, through shambles and lanes, catching a glimpse every so often of the disguised fugitive. Soon they were traversing the stinking hovels that rimmed the outer edges of the town and there he was, slowed to a walking pace now, and he ducked into a low doorway and vanished.

Finn dismounted and walked towards the door. He could hear a baby crying in the distance and then another one from the doorway in front of him. As he stepped forward a familiar figure appeared in the doorway, and beckoned him in with a wave. His heart missed a beat when he saw who it was. Enid.

"What are you doing here?" he asked, and then he realized this must be her home. She maintained her puzzling aura, and did not speak, but he knew to follow. Entering the dark hallway he followed her through to the kitchen area where a warm and welcoming fire blazed in the hearth. Gorgeous baking smells emanated from the range and he could see food prepared for a celebratory feast on the table.

"It's Moonday, Finn. A day to celebrate and be thankful for the life-force we all have, don't you know?"

The voice behind was quiet, and its owner, entering the room, was familiar. A sense of panic gripped Finn, for the owner of the voice was none other than Grindrod. Finn looked around the room making sure of his escape, trying to locate the best door to run from, feeling for a weapon, and still looking out for his rescuer.

But, Grindrod looked different. He seemed relaxed, serene and peaceful. He was now dressed in bright colours and wore a floppy woollen hat, and a long smock, just like the man who was attacked by the guards. He smiled at Finn, trustingly, inviting him into his world.

"People like us have a feast day, every Moonday. We have all our friends and neighbours round and share. We have to keep it quiet though or, you know, He might come for us too."

"I have a very difficult life you know, trying to make ends meet, pretending to be loyal, saving a few souls along the way…. here, sit down, you have had a narrow escape. You need this."

As they ate, Grindrod explained how he had looked after him and his brother, and how Finn's Mother had helped with the cover to allow him to fool The Guardian and keep his employment.

"She has some of Murchadh's skills, you know," he helpfully explained.

Life in the dungeons was difficult, but because of The Guardian's lack of attention to the detail, his laissez faire attitude, Grindrod could go about his real business as a saver of souls.

Over the meal Grindrod was a fount of knowledge. The Guardian, he explained between mouthfuls of a lentil and bean pie, had once been very powerful, as Dara had told Finn already, but now was trapped in the confines of the Castle and the Homelands. His previous experience in battle and his empire building past made him restless. He blamed anyone and everyone for his incarceration, but laid the blame most squarely on Finn's head, as the apparent real heir to the kingdom, since Finn's family had cursed him somehow. For no other reason than a whim, he had taken an intense dislike to a sect of religious tolerants, the Zephyrine, who practiced peace and harmony and tried to bring contentment to the Homeland. They had a strong influence on the Homelands, being mystical, unlike the Selfists. Regardless of the size of their community, their power could keep The Guardian firmly in check. Not only could he not leave the Homeland, but he was unable to muster enough force to expand the empire he so ruthlessly wanted. The more it expanded, the weaker he became, so losing a battle became a salve for his illness.

He had however found a terrifying solution to his problem. Annihalation of the Zephyrine would reduce their power, and eventually allow him to break out of the prison; and expand his dwindling empire. So he set out to systematically destroy them, every last one.

"And that," he said, "includes me, and Enid, and, more relevant to you, your Mother. Of course that also makes you one too, although you don't realise that yet. So, he will come for you in the end. And only you can defeat him."

The meal ended soon for Finn, and with these words ringing in his ears he set off to find his brother. This could be difficult as he was still in the Castle. He determined that the simplest way was for Enid to come with him, and for her to sneak into the Castle by one of her secret entrances. This plan held obvious dangers, but it was the only way to get to his Mother. Enid may have known part of the way there, but only Dara knew the exact route. Arriving back up at the Castle, Finn lurked in the grounds, pointing to Enid where she might find Dara. To his chagrin, she already seemed to know where he would be, and she stealthily set off towards the Castle, disappearing from sight in an instant.

He moodily cursed Dara under his breath, their sibling rivalry not far from the surface. It seemed to be hours he waited, but in the fullness of time he saw the two of them appearing from the Castle, arm in arm as though they were not so secret lovers, chatting nonchalantly. This was an act, although Finn was not aware, and he cursed again. Dara clicked his fingers confidently, and a squire appeared with his horse. The two of them mounted the horse together, Enid in Dara's arms. He smiled at her, and they gazed in each other's eyes. Then they galloped off.

"What the hell was that about?" Finn said, trying to control his deep felt anger. "Look, Dara we need to go back to Mother's," he said with resolve. "We need to find out what to do."

Grimly, Dara agreed, and they set off in the direction of the Forest, taking Enid with them. Grindrod had decided she would be safer there, as The Guardian may have spotted them together, and all agreed this was a good idea.

10 The Mission

"Well, Finn, we had better get down to business, then," Finn's Mother finally said, after finishing her tea.

"You need to go and find your father, it's as simple as that. Only you can do it. I can't leave here, and there is no one else. I do have a map, which shows where he was last seen. You must keep it very well hidden. If it falls into the wrong hands then we are all in serious trouble."

Finn gathered the 'all' she referred to was a bigger all than just the assembled group here.

"Do you understand how important this is? We need him back. We need him to get rid of The Guardian once and for all, and we need him now. Our kind is dwindling and soon we will all be gone. Then, nothing could stop him."

A thousand questions raced through Finn's mind. The most important was; "Why does this have to be me?" but there seemed no way of asking that without looking scared or just not interested. His Mother answered as though she had heard him ask out loud..

"Finn, dear, He can't control you. Everyone else he can affect. He has the power to take over their minds, their bodies, make them do his bidding, even make them become traitors. They can't help it, no one can. I'm well hidden, but if I came out of cover he would be sure to find me. And we can't have that can we?"

Finn looked slightly less concerned but was still churning inside. His Mother proceeded to rummage about in a chest, hidden in a dark corner, and brought out four items. One was the map she had referred to, and the others were a large burgundy coloured cloak with leather trimming, a pack of playing cards, and last of all was a bag of fruit.

"I know it's a lot to ask, but you need to leave the Homelands and bring him home. Here is the plan. It shows a safe route out of the confines of the Homelands. Your Father will know the way back, so the plan will....dissolve, the image change, as you move through it to disguise its true nature."

"It shows your Father at the Five Fathoms Inn in a town called Watersedge, by the Emerald Ocean. Of course, he may not be there now so you need to find the Innkeeper. He, or She, of course, will send you in the right direction. You must be very careful to talk to the right person. They will be suspicious, so please don't be flippant with them."

"And yes, before you ask, you do need to take Dara along with you. You need all the help you can get," she announced. As if he hadn't already thought of that.

"What is this?" asked Finn, puzzled by the new cloak. "Some kind of invisibility cloak or something?"

"Don't be stupid Finn, you only get that sort of thing in fairy tales! No, but you can keep warm in it. You will find it has some other useful properties. It was Murchadh's, after all. And it's big enough for you both to fit under."

"What about these?" he said looking quizzically at the cards.

"Just keep them by you. They will occupy you when you're bored, and you never know when they might come in handy. And the fruit is to eat, of course." Their Mother had always been the practical sort and she maintained this admirable trait even in the face of impending adversity. Finn thought about it and decided that this practicality was a nervous reaction to transpiring events; therapy, kind of.

"Right; when you find your Father he will know it is time to return. He has been waiting for a signal for many years now. Good luck Finn, and you Dara, we all depend on you. You have to succeed…"

The two boys, feeling insignificant and ever so slightly afraid, packed their belongings and set off on horseback looking back only once as their Mother waved to them in tears. Enid sat dejectedly on the ground beside her feet, in the leaves and earth, her beautiful elfin face buried in her milk-white hands, the slender fingers drumming on her forehead with tension and internal agony. In silence the two brothers looked at each other. The realism had finally dawned that they might never return, they might never see her again, and they might be on their last journey together.

With this thought running through his mind he left, waving good-bye, and made his way back through the town to Grindrod's house. He was feeling sad for himself now having all this responsibility, and he thought briefly how simple his life had actually been sitting in a wheelchair getting absolutely everything done for him. Now, he had the world on his shoulders, his brother to look after and the world to save, and it wasn't even lunchtime. Still, he obviously had his health back, and his family were all living and he had some ability to undertake all these challenges. These people had faith in him. He was important and could do it. He felt enervated and alive. He reminded himself, again, this could all be a dream so why not get on with it. It was still better than being pushed about all day long.

Just then he saw someone rushing towards him in a state of panic, with bruising over his face. It was one of Grindrod's neighbours, a man he recognised from the family feast, but only because of his bright green tunic.

"Finn McGarrigle?" he shouted, and when Finn identified himself the man shook and stammered. "They've captured Grindrod! You've got to escape from here, fast!"

"Where is he? What's happened to Grindrod?"

The questions as usual were seemingly without answer, and the man fled without providing any more responses.

"It will be too late for him, I am sure of it" said Dara his head bowed in gloom.

"But I need him. He's got things for me. He has to help…" shouted Finn, now fearful and confused. He needed help. He couldn't find the way himself. He needed guidance.

"I'll just have to find some way to get him out," he announced automatically, as though this was his mission. " You need to stay safe. I need you to help me find Dad. I need you alive. Ride around for a while then go back to the house. They won't expect anyone to be there after they have searched it. Hide out there; it's the safest place. And don't worry…I'll be back to get you later."

11 *Into the Lion's Den*

Finn rode purposefully back towards the Castle. He knew the way in. He knew the layout of the dungeons. He knew how to move around this Castle without being seen. He knew that The Guardian couldn't tell if he was there or not. It was his Castle, now. He was invisible, and more to the point he felt invincible.

Crossing the courtyard was the most difficult part. It was wide open and being the middle of the day there were crowds of people milling around. A market was on and stalls littered the area. Good cover, thought Finn, as he crept closer, having left his horse tied up back in town. He had no weapons, but knew he didn't need them. He was Captain Invincible. He could walk and run, now. He could do it.

Or could he? Indecision haunted him momentarily, but he shook it off. The comfortable life he had back home began to look inviting. Even in a wheelchair, he had everything he wanted and was always safe. But real or not he couldn't be hurt. He knew this in his bones.

Hiding behind a pile of barrels, he looked carefully at the route, choosing his strategy with care. His strategy involved running wildly across the courtyard, right through the milling crowd at the market and in the main doors. Unbelievably, it worked.

Once inside he kept close to the walls, listening carefully and looking out for The Guardian. He was nowhere to be seen. Finn ran down the stairs trying to avoid Percival but, of course, he couldn't. Fearing he had been rumbled, he stopped, and Percival simply said; " I have been looking for you; your rooms are a mess and the servants are complaining, mainly to me. And you missed breakfast. I, of course, will be in terrible trouble if you don't eat properly." A small tear formed in his eye, with the fear and worry of what The Guardian might do to him.

Finn promised he would eat soon and told him not to worry, saying he was on his way up to his room to help clear up. "Why was it in a mess?" he thought. He got back to the task in hand as Percival wheeled off and disappeared from view, and he walked slowly and deliberately down to the dungeons.

Just then a large group of Orphans ran bustling past him and straight towards the dungeons, almost pushing him over as they ran. The last one stopped and looked round at him, grinning wildly and encouraging him to come, with a shake of his head in the direction of the rest. Finn joined the group, running. A perfect disguise he thought; hiding out amongst a group of invisible children. As they approached the dungeons the door burst open and The Guardian stormed past, angrily shaking a fist and shouting incoherent abuse at the feral children. He turned, and fuming, stalked past Finn without even seeing him. Finn just about fainted seeing him so close and dangerous.

The group continued running and went straight through the dungeons. Finn somehow knew that Grindrod would be in the fifth room along and he stopped briefly to check through the tiny grate. His hunch was right, but at that moment a burly guard pushed him away with the wooden end of a pike.

Just then the Orphans turned, and as one screaming, swooping mass they descended on the guard, smothering him as they clambered over his collapsing body and trampling him into the stone floor of the corridor. Finn instantly became one of them and they were a protective mass army, acting as one. Finn took his chance as he saw the keys on the guard's belt through the writhing mass of kids. He stretched in and grabbed them. But the guard wasn't totally finished. He grabbed Finn's hand and squeezed hard. Just then sharp teeth sank into the guard's wrist and he screamed in agony as the flesh tore. He let go quickly and Finn snatched the keys and ran to the torture chamber as quickly as he could, fumbling with the lock.

The door swung open and he was greeted with the sight of a slumped broken body. Grindrod, right enough. He checked him out and found him barely alive. Untying him from the chair, his body slumped. Finn tried to pick him up, but his lifeless body was just too heavy.

"How do I move this?" he thought. " How can I get him home?"

And as if to answer, the feral writhing mass of kids snaked into the room and picked him and the body up on their spindly arms and carried them out of the door, out of the dungeons and out into the open air through a grated exit, which was presumably used normally to bring unfortunates into these rooms under the cover of dark.

"Where is everyone?" thought Finn, but then he saw the heaped and broken bodies of the guards, slumped around the exit and he knew a stronger force had helped him here. He hid the body behind a trough and went for his horse. Somehow he managed to get Grindrod up from the ground and on to the back of his horse, and he leapt up and headed off as fast as his beast could carry him. Where to was the problem. He stopped off at Grindrod's house and called for Dara, who fortunately was still there. Groaning audibly, Grindrod managed to direct him to a trunk containing the items he was to take with him. They seemed trivial. There was the ubiquitous sword, which seemed a bit on the short side, to be frank. It was a long black skean dubh, with Celtic symbols woven in silver on its hilt. There was a blanket, which was a tartan, predominantly sumptuous dark green in colour, which Finn somehow recognised as a Campbell tartan, and he wondered about the connotations of this cloth, representative of the murderous clan, in league with the supposed enemy of the people, duplicitous and scheming; invited to a banquet and killing their hosts. Perhaps it meant something different, or even nothing, here in this strange land.

There was a brass compass, dulled with age and in need of a good polish, and there was finally an impressive timepiece. That's the best word he could think of to describe it...which seemed to have its mechanism on the outside, and where you looked through a thick rounded glass lens into the clock to see the time, except there were thirteen hours shown, seven hands, and no numbers, but strange lettering instead.

They had to get away, though, and there was no time to think about these things now. Fortunately, there was a sack with pockets, a gadget bag, into which the items fitted perfectly, side by side, cosily cuddled up to each other, but seemingly weightless much to Finn's relief, as he slung the full bag over his shoulder.

Last of all Grindrod pressed a small blue stone firmly into Finn's hand.

"I won't be needing this now, but you do," he said weakly, and fainted. Finn looked at the stone, which glowed faintly in his hand and seemed to hum with power. He immediately put it in his pocket and set about business.

Finn and Dara picked themselves up and took the opportunity to use the cover of the fading light to carry Grindrod to the only place they knew he would be safe; their Mother's cottage, in the clearing. Finn might have been in charge, and he felt the power of a leader, but he was not in possession of all the information.

"Where is it Dara?" he had to ask.

"I'll tell you if you use the *magic* word," his brother answered him, with a defiant twinkle in his eye. However, he gulped visibly when he saw the serious look on Finn's face.

"Stop messing about and tell me where it is, or I might come up with a few magic words you wont like…."

"It's this way," Dara said quickly, and as Finn's frown relaxed into a grin they both laughed, for the first time in hours. Somehow they knew things would work out fine, but even so their fingers were metaphorically crossed in hope…. And so, they set off, this time Finn being completely aware of the route he followed. It seemed less important now to keep the secret, now that their world was in turmoil.

As they arrived at the cottage, the door was already open, and Enid was standing silently in the open doorway, a look of abject misery on her face. Finn's Mother stood behind her, her hands resting comfortingly on Enid's shoulders.

"Bring him in," she said. " We shall get him into a bed for some rest. He'll be safe here. Dara get the kettle on. Right now, we need some tea."

12 The Journey Starts

Leaving, this time for the last time, they felt resolve and responsibility. The route they had to follow took them dangerously close to the town; this town with its towering Castle which had become so familiar to him and which he now, even after this short time, or had it been his entire life, regarded as home. It was far from his dank, dreary home of the past and of his misfortunate, miserable other self. Here, he was a King. A sullen, disaffected King, but in a way it was better than being pushed around in a wheelchair, imprisoned in a metal trolley with no control over his life. Here, he had complete control, even if he didn't quite know what to do with it yet. But even so, he knew when the time came he would know what to do. Intuition led him to know that, here, he had been trained for the life of a warrior, even though the skills were elusive and imperceptible to him now.

Bizarrely, there were no signs of any guards on the route, and they crept stealthily through the sparse outskirts of the town without being noticed. Or so they thought, but out of their vision, curtains twitched nervously, and unseen eyes peered out and followed them, as they headed into the distance and into the forest, now chatting jokily about the events that might happen. Gallows humour had taken hold and they laughed about the possibility of being captured by trolls and beating them on the head from the height of their saddles, hitting them with clubs and watching them run for the hills, or having to fight some vicious sheep on the moors. They laughed now, but what if the sheep were vicious?

The darkness of the forest canopy gave them welcome shade from both the bright sunlight and from any prying eyes that might be out there. As twilight came, and the feeble sun disappeared behind the horizon, the two moons shone brightly, and they decided to camp for the night. Enough had happened today.

After finally tying up the horses, and making a very small and hopefully, unnoticeable fire to cook on, they collapsed in a collective heap on the ground, shattered. The burgundy cloak was indeed big enough for both of them and as lost boys they clung together for warmth and company under it. Best friends, brothers in arms. Soon both were asleep, soundly. But not for long.

The horses sensed it first and became restless, pacing around and snagging themselves on their reins, which were tied not too securely to spindly branches. These soon snapped and the horses cleared out. The two boys woke with a start, and realising the horses were loose got up and chased after them, talking soothingly to reassure them. The horses were not reassured, however, and soon it became evident why, as, snaking through the undergrowth, loudly rustling the fallen leaves as they moved, came a strange weaving creature. Two, now four, then more.

They looked exactly the same as normal, everyday brown earthworms, but each was about four feet long, and had wide-open jaws with sharp, worrying teeth. Hideously, they had no sign of any other facial features. They looked as though they were screaming but they uttered no sound. Finn and Dara made up for the lack of sound and screamed at the top of their voices. It was clear to Finn that these beasts were new to Dara, as he seemed to be even more scared by the sight of them. They followed their instinct and jumped up onto the horse's backs. This spooked the horses more and they reared up, stamping on the worms as they came down. The unfortunate creatures burst in a shower of fluids, pus and blood, pouring from their ruptured skin. But there were more of them. Suddenly it became clear that these worms were not on the attack, as several of them blithely slipped passed the terrified party and on into the forest. No, these creatures were running from something even more frightening.

And then it appeared, bursting through a bank of bushes, snarling and screaming and growling, fangs bared in an enormous jaw, an array of gleaming white sharp teeth, dripping with frothy saliva and licked by an equally frightening black, lolling tongue. It had arrived in a rolling four-footed gait, but on coming across something more appetising than the super-worms it stopped, considered, and stood on its hind legs, reaching a full eight feet tall in the process. It seemed aware; not a wild, raging beast, and it took in its surroundings carefully, sizing up the opportunities. Then it leapt at Dara from a full twenty feet away and knocked him to the ground. He screamed and scrambled to his feet trying to escape from the frightening creature, which stopped and turned and moved in for the kill.

Finn had scrambled from his horse when he had the chance as the beast was occupied with his brother. He did the only and first thing he could think of, and grabbed the voluminous new cloak and threw it with all his might at the beast, in the dim hope of distracting it long enough for him to think of something else.

Whilst the cloak moved through the air in just the right direction it seemed to float airily towards its target in slow motion, spreading out and rotating as if flew. The beast looked round and seemed to laugh, raising its enormous hairy head high in the air and snarling loudly, its pointed ears standing to attention. And then the cloak fell squarely over it, and it was enveloped in darkness. The snarl turned to a roar; a growling roar of fear and hatred.

The last of the worms careered past and into the darkness of the forest, the horses bolted and the three were left alone, triangulated. Dara was a pile of uselessness, a quivering wreck waiting to die. The beast was swirling round trying to get the cloak off its back, the mass of material wrapped itself around the beast's body and as it twisted the material seemed to twist too, growing and tying itself in ever tightening knots as the beast writhed, becoming strangled, and it was soon scared too. The growl, the roar was noticeably turning to a squeal of panic.

Finn suddenly realised he was standing motionless watching the cloak do all the work for him. Fear was subsiding, as he knew he had a chance to dispatch the creature. He grabbed the long skean-dubh from his waistband, carefully taking it from its sheath, and he purposefully marched towards the confused creature, and plunged the cool metal blade deep into the writhing cloak. There was a howl of agony, and the cloak stopped moving. The creature turned and ran. As it did, the cloak unwrapped itself and fell lifeless onto the ground, pulling the blade with it. It fell with a noisy satisfying clang on the ground, hitting off a rocky outcrop and flashing as it did so, sparking in the darkness. Finn looked at the blade, which glowed pleasingly in the forest floor. As he watched the terrified creature run for cover, he picked it up and placed it back in his sheath for another day. He suddenly remembered to breathe and exhaled noisily, whooping and cheering and calling out in exhilaration. After all, he had just saved Dara's life.

His brother remained still, motionless; literally petrified. But he was at least alive. Finn shook him into life and they grabbed each other, hugging in the pure joy of life.

"I think you've stood in something," said Dara looking at the mess of worm innards on Finn's shoes, and he laughed in relief. Finn grimaced at the mess, wiping his foot on the ground.

"We have to move, quickly," said Finn, assertively. "Pick up your stuff. We'll find the horses and get on our way. I don't really feel like sleeping now," he added, understating the obvious.

Fortunately, the horses had enough sense to stay nearby, and were soon corralled. They appeared to be relieved too, if that could be discerned from their behaviour, and once gathered up, the two boys went on their way again, silently in the dark, the sound of owls hooting in the distance forming a strange reassuring backdrop, a sound of normality in the frightening scary dark place they now found themselves, alone.

13 *Onwards*

Worn out, exhausted but resolute, they made their way through the forest, leaving its confines soon after dawn, relief visible on their faces as they escaped the rampaging wolf-bear-man-creature, whatever it was, and the slightly disturbing toothed worms which they had since decided were basically harmless but not the kind of thing you might bring home as a pet.

The threat of all forests is the dark corners where anything could be lurking, waiting for the unwary traveller. It could be wild animals, it could be unseen traps in the forest floor, it could be other people, and it usually was; highwaymen taking advantage of the cover the forest could provide to ply their evil and dastardly trade. So far so good; only mythical, wild beasts to deal with. In some ways these were more predictable than violent humans, Finn mused as they left the forest canopy. Before them was a beaten track heading through lush green rolling hillsides. Finn couldn't help but think the highwaymen might prefer this terrain. At least they were safe from monsters out here. He decided they should stop and rest awhile, since they had no sleep last night, and who knows what they might have to deal with on the road ahead.

They stopped and unwrapped the food they had brought, and emptied their canteens of water. Fighting demons caused a dreadful thirst, they agreed.

"How about a game of cards?" asked Finn, not entirely sure he wanted to indulge, himself.

Dara nodded affirmative, so Finn rummaged around his bag and pulled them out. He thought about a game of rummy, explained the rules to Dara who had never heard of this game, and started to shuffle the cards. He had soon dealt out his seven, and Dara's eight, and put the rest in between them face down.

Both picked up their cards to assess their hands, but then looked dumbfounded at them. They looked at each other suspiciously.

"Are all your cards completely different?" Finn piped up finally. " I mean no spades or hearts or…. But you wont have these here will you?"

"Lets look at them first," said Dara practically. So they turned over their cards. Each was completely dissimilar to the others, and instead of suites of numbers, with kings and queens and jacks, they each had a twisted face on them, and a title written underneath in runic or dwarfish or something else Finn could not decipher. He counted them. Fifty-one.

"What use are fifty one unreadable different cards?" He was about to throw them away when he remembered his Mothers words and thought better.

"I'll just keep them in my bag, then," he said.

They sat metaphorically twiddling their thumbs in silence for some time. As they sat, they saw a train of people heading their way in the opposite direction. It moved slowly and there were people on foot and there were horses pulling carts. They decided to brazen it out and wait by the roadside, attempting not to draw attention to themselves, but also there seemed nowhere to hide in this open area, and the very act of hiding might create suspicion. When the raggle-taggle train reached them they saw that it comprised the walking wounded from some battle.

A man was playing a musical instrument, similar to a jews harp, twanging it at his mouth as he walked, quite tunelessly, and another endlessly quoted some poetry; to pass the time, and perhaps to stay awake or even alive.

"High upon the hill, silhouetted by the sky, we watched in deathly silence as the warriors marched by….by night they marched, the dark passed by, to Croí Dorchadas where they would die."

This was a defeated army, uninterested in two healthy and wealthy looking travellers; the dregs of mankind, beaten and broken, depressed and dejected. Halfway through the group someone finally noticed them and bade a half-hearted welcome.

"Morning, guv'nors," the crumpled man said, blood encrusting an open wound on his face. "Or should I say, your Lordships?" He had obviously realised who they were. Of course, they were the most well known faces in the Homelands and this should have been no surprise to them. He stopped to speak to them.

"Wot you doing out here?" he asked. " You can probably gather that things aren't going quite so well just now. These are the ones who *can* get away. We've left hundreds, maybe thousands, behind. Some vile new weapon they've got. We just can't cope. It's horrible; it's terrible; it's awful, I simply can't describe it."

As he spoke they looked at the hollowness and the distant sadness in his eyes.

"We'll be sent back, you know…. He doesn't care how many die. But then, neither of them do. Can't you say something to Him? Help us, please. We can't go on like this you know."

Finn was speechless as he looked at the inhuman traffic passing him, limbs missing, groaning, vomiting. Some were dying there and then, and they were simply thrown off the carts to make it easier for those having to pull them. It was, he admitted uneasily, horrible. No words could express this, and in his short life he had never seen anything like it. He had had his troubles. He had experienced the pain these men were going through, but he still couldn't empathize properly. Someone did this to them, deliberately… but again, without any real malice, in a way. It was dog eat dog out there.

Obviously, it was war and the combatants couldn't know who they were damaging, but each one must know deep inside that what happened to their colleagues, was happening to the other side, and the consequences were clear. Why didn't they just stop?

At least the idiot who had maimed him was only that; an idiot who had no idea he would kill when he left his home that evening, he hadn't planned anything. It just happened. But then again he should have seen the consequence of his irresponsibility. He could have got the bus after all…and he had died too. What a waste of two lives. Finn looked into the imploring empty eyes, and, biting his lip, he did all he could; he lied.

"I'll see what I can do," he said, knowing he would never have the influence with The Guardian this poor bloke thought he might. And he was going in the opposite direction. If he had to cross this battlefield then he might not even get to change things. The chill thought of the enemy suddenly crossed his mind.

"It might have been my Dad who did this to these men", he thought with dread.

"Look, things are going to change," he said to the broken man. "I'm trying to stop the carnage. That's my mission. But…." And he took this man into his confidence and said clearly to him " …you mustn't tell anyone you met us, or I wont be able to stop this…."

"Where are you going guv'nor? Why aren't you back at the Castle, safe and sound? What's going on?" The man said now, puzzled by their presence in this strange place beyond the safety of the Homelands, beyond hope. And suddenly, without any warning, he keeled over and died, right there on the spot. As he fell it was evident that a massive tear in his side was dripping blood and this wound, and the slow interminable loss of life-force, had conspired to kill him. Finn caught him as he fell, and with the man's blood on his hands, he lowered him gently to the ground, stunned by the shock. Dara gaped at him, speechless.

A few of the train of death looked over, and each with their own empty eyes laid the blame fairly and squarely on these pampered princes, but their perverted loyalty prevented them from saying anything. A few others fell on the way and the train moved on, heading for home, the inhuman remains being left at the roadside for the wolves to get later. Carrion would pick the bones clean and the evidence would soon be destroyed.

Left watching at the roadside, as the stragglers finally passed into the distance, Finn was now feeling ashamed of his apparent luxury, and his complicity in the death around him. He resolved to do what he could to stop it once and for all. He was the heir to the throne after all, and if anyone could do something about it, it should be him.

With a heavy sigh he turned to Dara and beckoned him over. Dara was still stunned looking; his gaping mouth unable to close, his mind unable to comprehend how terrible it might be out there. Privilege, luxury, conspicuous consumption; the ordinary things he took for granted seemed extravagant and worthless now as he thought about these soldiers wasted on the pyre of greed and folly.

"Lets get to work," Finn said, and Dara nodded, understanding immediately that they had to stop this, or no one else would.

As they travelled on, Dara was silent. His usual, good-natured, gabbling self, joking and laughing, had been replaced by a miserable clone, unable to raise a smile or hold a conversation. Travelling on they soon had to stop, and Finn fell into the deepest sleep he had for many months.

14 Interlude

The blackness, a dark void, a chasm, welcomed him. He opened his eyes and found himself somewhere else, horribly familiar. Home, bed, his old room. He listened to the silence in the darkened room. Outside his door he could hear the sounds of suburban 21st century life. Traffic sounds, horns and screeching tyres, a dog barking loudly in the distance at a flock of fleeing seagulls, a baby crying as its rattly, clanky frog shaped toy fell slowly from its grip and out of the confines of its buggy, a couple across the way were arguing loudly with each other, a train hauntingly sounded its horn at the level crossing two miles away. It was playtime at the local primary school and the kids were an agglomeration of screaming noise in the distance, and an obscenity could be heard liquidly floating through the grimy fume filled air from a group of vile teenagers running across the road in front of a Volkswagen Golf. Silence, peace.

What started with a heaving sigh of relief then paled as he remembered his legs, or more to the point lack of legs. He looked down and felt them. He tried to move but couldn't and crying silently was soon heaving himself across the bed, and he fell onto the floor with a resounding thud.

Worried footsteps could be heard running down the hall, and the familiar face of his Dad, dressed in his best meeting suit, with a new unironed shirt and tie, poked his head round the door. Yet it was unfamiliar. He had a beard now; his face seemed more pointed than he remembered, a bit more devilishly handsome.

"You rang?" he said trying to be light, as he saw the crumpled mess of Finn on the floor.

"We'll soon get you back into bed. Was that a bad dream? You've had quite the adventure, haven't you? Right now, I've got an interview for a new job closer to home, so I can take care of you. Fingers crossed. I'll be back to see to you later. You stay exactly where you are. I'll be back for you."

Finn's head swam with confusing thoughts. He couldn't quite work out which of his lives was reality now. This one just didn't feel real enough, but then he was only half the person here.

He soon heard a car door slam shut and the muffled sound of the exhaust, and soon it disappeared into the distance. He was back in silence listening to the 21st century outside his window. Early summer; birds and bees, buzzy insects, and general noise. Presently a whistling person came up the path to the house and it was clear to Finn this was Dara, returned from a hard day doing normal teenage things with his friends. The whistling stopped before the door was opened and there was a strange conspiratorial silence, and the implied feeling that there was more than one person here. The door creaked slowly open.

"Finn, it's just me!" said Dara's bright cheerful voice. But again there was the feeling this was acting, that he was saying this not for Finn's benefit, but for someone else, someone worrying. Stifled footsteps were coming up the stairs and there were definitely two sets of them. Finn was getting scared, as he had no way of escape, no way of running. He couldn't even get out of bed, for Gods sake…the handle turned excruciatingly slowly.

As it opened Finn slunk under the covers. Dara appeared at the door. He seemed bigger than before and filled the door menacingly.

"Am I paranoid?" thought Finn, as if, well… he thought, paranoid.

Then he saw there was a second person, and his fear grew. But his fear subsided when he saw the second person enter the room. A slight elfin figure entered the room and busily fussed about him. Enid.

"Finn, we have to move you quickly, it's not safe here," she said in a small, whispery voice. He could hear an accent. Scandinavian? Irish? Scottish? He couldn't place it. Finn was taken aback at the voice. It swam round his head and it was elusive and invisible, but he knew she had spoken at last. Dara lifted him from the bed and carried him down the stairs. They were followed by Enid, who seemed in charge. She followed, and sprinkled water on all the surfaces they touched as she went.

"This will ensure He can't follow us," she said confidently and breathily.

Once in his wheelchair, they ran from the front door and down the street. This was the familiar, homely scene he had known for his whole life, apart from the obvious. A burning red sky above him. Two shadowy moons, still visible in the daylight.

Then, suddenly, his home was in flames. Against the red sky it seemed normal. From nowhere a car came screeching along the road, the bearded pointy man who seemed to be Dad, no longer Dad. Enid threw a bottle of the water at the windscreen as it approached close and the car spun off into the roadside stopping abruptly, with smoke streaming from the window. More flames and the face screaming in agony.

Run, run like the wind…Dara was strong and those years of sports (or was it tournaments and horse riding?) came in very handy now. Then the surroundings dissolved and they were back in the Homelands, or somewhere close. He saw the old wizened man from the steps again, beckoning, 'Quickly, Quickly!' And then he was tipped from the chair and falling once more. He hit the ground and it gave way. The grass opened up and swallowed him. The blackness, the void, the chasm were here again.

What was happening? And again, he blacked out, as the realisation and relief came that this was just a bad dream.

15 *The Battlefield of Lyre*

They travelled on for two full days; Dara in total silence, Finn left with his own thoughts, but planning strategy all the way. Dara grunted occasionally in response to queries about his health, his sanity, or if he was hungry. Finn still had the horrible feeling that his Father might have become as evil as The Guardian. That this war was one of mutually assured destruction with stakes being raised all the time, and the original aims of the conflict forgotten. To win the battle, the good side, whatever that meant and it was usually the side you were on, had to lower their values and fight as dirty as the other side.

His abiding, some might say obsessive, interest in the Second World War gave him all sorts of parallels. Look at 'Bomber' Harris and the bombing of Dresden, and more to the point; Hiroshima, and Nagasaki. Think of all the innocent bystanders caught up in the conflict there. If Japan had done that would it be a war crime? But we were the winners so it was justified. And what about the fact that they were two different bombs and it seemed now to be all part of some hideous experiment to try out two different weapons.....but on the other hand look at the Holocaust, and look at the Japanese Prisoner of War camps. He had heard the story of his Great Uncle and what being captured by the Japanese had done to him. But for all of this conflict, he realised he was no pacifist. If it had to be done, he would do it. His idealism came from a different direction. Truth, purity and other lofty ideals. He sounded like Superman. His youthful naivety might make these laughable when said out loud, but he was on the right track and he knew it. Time would mould them into a philosophy.

His mind was swimming with conflicting thoughts and he could hardly sleep at night. It was utterly depressing and all part of the human condition, he thought. His only hope was that he could make a difference. Speak to his Father, depose The Guardian and the Homeland could live happily ever after. It was all that easy. He laughed sardonically, aloud, at this naïve hope. Dara stared at him sullenly.

On the third day, late in the evening twilight, they arrived. And it was worse than they had imagined. The Battlefield of Lyre, it transpired, had been the site of a battle for twenty-five years, or more. Each side had built a network of earthwork trenches and they could not advance from these permanent structures. These were no more than 500 metres from each other, and the combatants could shout obscenities at each other. There were numerous banners raised above the trenches abusing the enemies mothers, and if they were lucky, girlfriends; for this was a young battle force, the least capable of complaining; the youth, a wasted, doomed youth.

Each side was taking turns at lobbing massive fireballs of flaming hay at each other. These would split on landing and hidden glass jars filled with burning oils would spew out into the trenches, maiming and burning those in the vicinity. Generally, the weapon of choice seemed to be crossbows but in order to use these, men had to rise above the trench walls and make them selves a target.

Small trained birds were also being used to drop missiles on the other side, but these were often captured and sent back with a similar payload; that was if they weren't eaten first. Rodents occupied the trenches and there were thousands more of these than there were soldiers. These, presumably, caused disease and death on a greater scale than the enemy fire could.

Finn and Dara first saw the battlefield from high above on a hillside, and they winced in empathy with the agony of the soldiers below. It was pure hell, with the flying firebombs whistling incessantly in both directions, each briefly lighting up the arena as bright as floodlights, before exploding, surreally making it look like an exciting sports match. Finn could even imagine a commentary, the trivialisation of the carnage, being broadcast to the wider audience. They didn't have TV here, of course, but if they did would this be the entertainment?

The audience back home had no idea what was going on here, and only responded to reports carefully tailored by the authorities in the Castle, to make the battle seem noble, exciting, adventurous and justified. We were winning after all, weren't we? The train of death he had seen two days before belied this fact, though. As in the Tournament, a parade had been held every so often with fresh faced, bright youngsters enthusing about the fight, about the prospects for victory, or about the vileness of the enemy. Empty speeches, played out by actors. Finn found it hard to believe that the Homelanders just swallowed it, and were wound up in a similar enthusiasm, but then there were numerous historical examples, after all.

Surveying the scene below, lit up by these evil lanterns, they could not quite understand why no-one was directing events from this vantage point. They could see both sides clearly from this height; the weaponry, the troops, the kitchens and barracks set up to serve them, and more to the point the fact that the death and destruction was contained within an incredibly small area. This was an arena of death, and there seemed no logic to it.

In the fading light they could still see into the distance aided by the bright cheerful, wistful moons-light. On either side there was lush green fields that were lovingly tended by farmers, who must be supplying food and sustenance to the two battling armies. Cosy, rich looking farmhouses with carefully tended lawns could be seen clearly adjoining the battlefield. They looked extravagant, and he could imagine the wealth these farmers must be amassing, servicing a readily available market for their goods, right at their doors. A whole town was being constructed to service the war, and the shops and associated residences had an air of wealth. There were pubs and bakeries, butchers and barbers.

But also adjoining the battlefield were enormous cemeteries, mass unmarked graves filled with numerous unknown men who had been sacrificed for…what? Glory? Peace? Who knew any more? Horrifically, the ground in between the trenches was piled high with skeletons and fresh corpses, presumably the detritus of battles from long ago. No one could go out there and pick up these unfortunate victims and give them a dignified burial, so they stayed there to rot, or become a feast for the rodent population, which was immune to, and profited from, the battle. Just like the farmers and businesses adjoining, Finn mused. He knew he had to go down there though, but not just yet.

They decided to set camp for the night right there. It seemed the safest place. They agreed to take turns sleeping, and after two hours would swap over, guarding each other. Finn was acutely aware though that his brother had become decidedly flaky, and he was unsure if he was reliable in any way. But he needn't have feared, for soon Dara was fast asleep, dreaming of fluffy sheep, or games, or the light simple life he had until recently, and Finn sat biding his time in the light of the missiles, formulating strategy, working out plans, thinking blissfully about the beautiful but silent elfin face buried peacefully in a soft pillow at his Mother's cottage, and soon dawn was upon them and they both slept soundly, unaware of the scream of the battle. They remained unseen on the hillside by the forces massed downhill, oblivious of anything around them other than their futile battle.

Dawn woke them with a start, or rather with a poke in the ribs as an officious sounding knight dressed rather wonderfully in heavy chain mail and a gleaming tunic stood high over them. He kicked Finn, who winced in pain.

"And who the bleeding 'ell are you, Sonny Jim?" he asked angrily. " And why are you up here and not down there with the others. You too good for it? Eh Eh?"

It was clear to Finn, as he groggily came to that this was some sort of General, or Sergeant Major, or something, and he seemed to think he had deserters on his hands. Or worse, spies…

"Get on your feet and down that hill…. we'll see what's what when you get a real earful from Lord Ponsonby. He'll have you strung up for deserting your posts."

At this statement Dara laughed out loud. "Wait a minute! Ponsonby? Desmond Ponsonby? That jumped up pantry boy. I'll tan his backside with my sword edge, you know. And what's this Lord thing about? He was my footman last year!"

His laughter was short lived however as he was thoroughly walloped on the ear by the Regimental Sergeant Major.

"That hurt," Dara said, hurt and close to tears.

"Don't you evah talk about his Lordship like that, again," now red faced, wide-eyed man screamed. "People like you make me sick," he hissed. "Get down there, right now!"

He shouted this last statement right into Finn's ear. Finn closed his eyes tightly and took the verbal beating, but vowed silently to get his own back somehow.

Thinking that it was probably best to follow orders, (they were sure they could sort it out with Ponsonby) they set off down the hill towards the hellish Battlefield and the trenches, trailing their ever more frightened horses behind them.

"And leave them! Right there!" The voice ahead shouted. "We can't have our brave lads kicked to death by these stupid beasts can we? And we might be able to eat them later if they're not blown to smithereens, Eh ,Eh?"

Finn and Dara were frogmarched down the hill, right into the midst of the trenches. The smell was horrendous, the noise excruciating, and the stench of fear palpable. Missiles continued to rain overhead, and down here in the midst of it all they seemed even more terrifying and enormous. Flames engulfed whole sections of trench and the stench of rotting and burning flesh permeated the whole local area. The men in the trenches seemed immune to the fearful weapons, but Dara and Finn ducked and winced every time a noise seemed to indicate a missile might be heading their way. They found themselves being hauled through water filled trenches with soupy mud sloshing around their ankles. Soon they arrived at their destination.

A hole in the ground, differentiated from the rest of the squalor by a timber framed door, with a sign carefully written in a rough calligraphy styled font; '*Lord Ponsonby*' it proudly stated. The RSM knocked three times, paused, then knocked once more on the door, opened it and pushed the two prisoners in.

"Ahhh, Enders' so very, very nice to see you, again," said the inhabitant of the hole, which remained dry despite the external conditions. With sudden recognition and a faint smile, he saw the RSM had company. The room was bigger than one might think from the outside, had a antique stained four poster bed with a mosquito net in vivid lime green, and a pleasant table and chairs in the middle of the room, with a candlestick and a floral display in the centre.

Ponsonby stood next to the table and sniffed extravagantly at a single blue stem held at arms length and bending elegantly towards his protuberant nose. His eyes were closed in rapture. He wore a billowing white shirt, black Hussar style trousers with a red stripe down each leg ending in fabulously shining black leather boots with bright white steel buckles, and he had extravagantly long flowing locks. He could have been some Bohemian poet, the very image of a Lord Byron, thought Finn. To complete the romantic effect, he even had a pirate cutlass slung low at his hips.

Shelves lined the walls with select and carefully arranged ornaments and books, and a small, curiously orange rat scurried around a treadmill in a cage. The treadmill seemed to be wired up to a light bulb, which flickered and changed from green to red to blue to yellow, as the rat scampered on at variable speed.

"A little invention! Worthless, but you've got to keep yourself amused here, somehow," said Ponsonby, with a twinkle in his voice. " How about a drink? I've just acquired a very, very nice bottle of the best local red. Can't pronounce its name. It's simply heavenly, though…never tasted anything like it. Blueberries!" he enthused.

"My God, Ponsonby, you've changed a bit, haven't you?" said Dara with a faint air of disgust at this opulent exhibition. He remembered him as a slight nervous lad with sharply cut hair and a permanently runny nose.

"Got to move with the time, dear," said Ponsonby. " Great opportunities out here for those who want to grab them…opportunities that is…. Life as a footman, well it just wasn't for me. So given the chance to join up out here, and the patronage of your great Guardian; well, who could refuse?"

"Now a little bird tells me that you two are in a bit of a pickle, and I see another of those wonderful opportunities just across the horizon. For me at least. Just need to keep you here and, best, alive, I think, and in a few days we can get word home and return you safe and sound to the loving bosom of your family. Doesn't that sound just wonderful, just tickety boo….."

Another noisy crash and a missile flew overhead missing the trench by metres. Finn just about had a heart attack. Ponsonby looked anxiously at some shaking crockery on the topmost shelf.

"Just had that cleaned would be a waste if it were to get damaged, what?"

"How about some olives?" said Ponsonby, brightly, changing subject suddenly. When his guests declined he said, "No appetite? Oh well." And he picked one out of a bowl, savoured it, and spat out the stone.

"Ahh, just a minute," he said suddenly remembering something vital. "I've just got to send out an order for a hundred, no, lets make it two hundred, men to go over the top. Won't be a moment…." And in a little aside he confided, "Terrible waste, I often think, but then someone has to do it. There is procedure, after all, to follow…."

He ducked his head out the door and two minutes later there was a loud whistle, and the sound of scrambling feet, followed by screams of agony and yells of "Mother!!" as the two hundred souls were extinguished immediately by crossbow fire.

"It's absolutely beastly, you know," he said coming back in through the door to the peace and quiet of the glory hole. "The blighters seem to be using some sort of new acidic tip on their arrows these days. Don't know why we didn't think of it first….But then we've been working on the gas of course," he ruminated, shaking a snow globe ornament in his hand. Finn could see it featured Tower Bridge, and couldn't quite work this out.

"It simply ruined last Wintermas, you know. We sent an experimental cloud of bilious gas over to the enemy lines; should have made them all very sick and stopped them enjoying their dinner, but the treacherous blighters simply used an enormous fan and blew it back at us. Even I was sick. Still, it beat eating rat. At least it stopped poor Jeremy over there," he pointed with a shiny sharp knife at the rat in the cage, "…being eaten. So, results all round!"

Ponsonby was clearly mad, Finn thought. Picking up a furry green fig to peel with the knife and ducking as another missile flew overhead, the screams from his nearby, incinerated, comrades ringing in his ears, he continued pontificating.

"Yes, war maketh the man, cometh the hour and all that," he said. "Look at me, a humble and poor, yes poor, working boy with no prospects. Given the opportunity," He savoured this word which was clearly a favourite, " you can make a General. I stepped into the breach at just the right time you see. Able to make decisions quickly, it turned out, just what was needed."

"…. and obviously no conscience," thought Finn, keeping this to himself.

"Kept me safe and sound in this veritable vault," he said. "What a stroke of luck. Now what about you two? We can't have you absconding can we, but then we can't have our Crown Prince a prisoner…. It's simple" he added" Can I trust you not to run away?"

"What?"

"You heard, can I trust you not to run away?"

"Of course you can, I'm Finn McGarrigle, and my word is my bond," said Finn through slightly clenched teeth, trying not to let any hint of body language give this lie away.

"Okay, off you go. Find a bunk and get some sleep. We'll have to keep you safe, yes?"

The door was opened and the RSM stuck his head in. He was wearing a skull cap, black in colour with a spike on top.

"Very, very fetching my good man! Bravo! Good to see someone cares about his appearance in this sartorial desert! Now, please get my two friends some food and somewhere incredibly comfy to bunk down, oh and order another attack, right away, don't want to be seen to be slacking, particularly if reports are heading home, do we?"

The RSM, rolling his eyes upwards, looked askance at this. His eyes were now bulging at the idiocy of his leader, but he led the freed prisoners away down the trench, through the mud and squalor and to show them the mess, and find them a bunk. As they headed away, a flaming missile flew overhead, screeching, incandescent, and it flew directly through the framed door of Ponsonby's quarters, exploding immediately in a ball of flames and high pitched screams, which soon mellowed into a whimper. As they stood up the saw the RSM run back towards Ponsonby's rooms, thought 'opportunity', and ran for it.

Caked in mud, the same as all the others in the trench, they easily blended in and managed to match the rest of the chaotic mess of humanity running around in a futile manner. But they had some purpose, at least, and were soon retracing their steps back to the horses, which with a sigh of relief they found exactly where they had been left, uneaten.

With Ponsonby gone, presumably no one was in charge, and with communication being what it was, it would be some time before anyone knew or particularly cared that the prisoners had escaped. So they took the chance to go further, skirting round the battlefield and behind the luscious farms, avoiding the enemy lines completely and easily.

They travelled for a whole day without stopping and soon they were miles from the battle and were safe, if in unknown territory. Finn checked the map carefully and saw that they were roughly on course. They had to double back a bit to regain the right route, but at least nothing was in their way now. Again they decided to slow down and get some rest. The landscape ahead was now a bland empty desert vista, with scrubby plants and dunes and the occasional skeleton of an unfortunate animal, dead of heat exhaustion or starvation. The closest was particularly interesting as it was the size of a domestic cow, but had seven skeletal limbs remaining. One had to assume that one limb was missing, because seven limbs would be a peculiar number to deal with. It also had tusks. They sat next to the strange skeleton and drank from their refilled canteens.

Dara was reminded by the surroundings of a story he had heard, probably in the tales of Brother Meirion, '*The Sad but True Tale of the Lizard King*', and to fill the interminable time he decided to recount it to Finn, whom he knew would have forgotten it even if he had told him it before. It was like telling a joke, sometimes you just couldn't remember it no matter how hard you tried. So for Finn this story would be like a joke. In a way it was a joke for the appropriateness of the story would be totally lost on Finn.

Dara began under the burning bright sunlight asking if Finn was sitting comfortably, and setting a scene.

"In a far, far away kingdom, a sandy dusty place, a bit like this, there lived a King. I'll call him Norman for simplicity, because you wouldn't be able to pronounce his name if you tried. Anyway, he reigned over his kingdom benevolently, was loved by all his subjects; his citizens were content, there were practically never any wars to worry about because he got on absolutely fabulously with everyone. He lived a full court life, but he was miserable. He was bored, because whilst he lived in luxury, he had no imagination so could never think of anything worth doing.

From early childhood he had been mollycoddled and kept safe. He grew up with a safe and super-cautious life, and only ever saw the inside of the Palace nursery. Of course he read books that fuelled his imagination and he was told stories by nannies, and entertainers regularly visited the palace to keep him happy. He never saw his Father, the King, who was continually employed on affairs of state, and his Mother only saw him first thing in the morning. They were both, however, incredibly cautious, having lost their firstborn child; they wanted nothing to happen to their other child. They loved him dearly and as the Queen could have no more children he was very precious.

As he grew he saw his peers learning to joust, or riding far from home and taking part in initiation rites, some involving great hardship or pain.

One even involved having skewers stuck through the skin of your chest and being flung by an enormous catapult. Or so he had heard. Only then, would you be a true warrior; a real man.

King Norman grew up appreciating fine wines, art and food, although he never got to cook himself, for kitchens were dangerous, hot places. He was waited on hand and foot by an army of servants all of whom looked after his every need. A new pair of socks would appear for him each morning, the old pair gone and he would never know where they came from.

One day he decided enough was enough. He had to get a more adventurous life. After all, King Boris of Hadania had a machine which flew over cliffs, and enabled him to glide across the plains in chase of vultures; King John of Verberada regularly jousted to the death with captured enemy knights (he did find that tying their arms behind their backs assisted greatly in this feat); King Derek of O, rode vicious dragons for fun.

So he sat and thought of what he could do. But of course his cautious life made him unable to comprehend anything that might be suitable. He could think of riding a raft down the Rapids on the great Nasargrada river, but that would be easy, tied to the side of the boat; he could think of riding his greatest war horse on a conquest of a nearby tyrannised country, but he couldn't think of one. All his neighbours were friendly or just not there; he could think of taking a long boat trip to foreign lands and bringing back a new vegetable, but he remembered the seasickness he had in childhood. And he still hated eating vegetables.

Everything was easily dismissed. So he just stayed within the Palace, eating the finest food, quaffing fine wines and admiring his art collection, which was, of course, assembled for him to ensure he never left home.

One night he had a dream. He was a lizard scurrying across the desert floor in search of food. He felt hungry; something he had never experienced in real life, and he also needed water urgently. The sun beat down on his back and he ran across the dunes. But more to the point, he was free for once. The feeling was exhilarating. He was free of all the constraints of his Monarch's role. No responsibility other than surviving. But he was failing at this. He was at death's door, but even this was unusual and exhilarating for him.

Weakening, he came across the carcase of another recently deceased lizard. In order to survive, he had no option other than to eat it, and he was revitalised. This was an inspiration to him. With the rush of excitement, he woke suddenly from his dream, enlivened, and rushed down to his chambers to think about it's true meaning. By the following morning he had determined what he should do. He left the Palace, dressed in the simple robes of a servant and telling no one but that servant, slipped out of the grounds unseen. He kept with him only a small talisman, which showed his true identity, which the servant alone would recognise, should it be absolutely necessary; just in case.

Soon he was travelling into the dusty outback of the desert, and passing strange new people and watching unusual ritual events like the ritual destruction of a nomadic village, and the slaughter of warthogs and their curing for the long dark winter. He passed through villages and markets and learned how to barter the few goods he had for food and drink. The markets were bustling and often-dangerous places and life for the common people was cheap. He saw several apparent murders and beatings, over the smallest disagreements and felt that he did not really know his people. On one or two occasions he barely escaped a beating himself as he carried the most ridiculous goods for barter. Gemstones and golden coins, which to him seemed natural, but to the commoners, looked like fakes.

Bruised and beaten he escaped into the depths of the desert and vowed not to return to the towns again, until he had learned how to live like the commoners and to fight back. He could not fail, and sought out the assistance of travelling soothsayers who plied their trades across the desert wastelands. But he was not an accomplished tracker, having never been taught these skills, and he was weak as he was never trained in stamina building exercises, and soon he was hopelessly lost as he had never been taught how to navigate by the sun or stars, and this was always done for him. Within days he was dying, in desperate need of food and drink, and he lay on the ground hallucinating. A man passed by on a camel and found him lying on the ground in the jaws of death. He gave him some water, but only after he had bartered it for the last remaining handful of gemstones, his shoes… and the talisman.

The stranger went on his way, refusing to divulge the true direction in which Norman should be travelling, even if Norman had been able to think about asking for such information. Norman was left to die once more. He had his ultimate freedom and the thrill of real life, and he crawled through the desert like a lizard only much more slowly.

Collapsing once more, the sustenance not being nearly enough, he lay baking in the sun. Just as in his dream, he noticed ahead of him the small decayed body of a dead lizard. If I can reach that he thought, I will survive.

He stretched out and grabbed at the body but it fell to pieces in his hand; dry, lifeless, worthless. And alone in the desert he died.

In this land, the souls of the dead travelled to their homes; the place they felt most happy; and he found himself in his nursery at home, where all those years before his promising full life had been curtailed on the death of his brother. His brother, only ever referred to as Pip, was also there, but of course could not possibly recognise him since he was thirty seven, and his brother a two year old. His brother played with the nursery toys and, smiling at them, ignored him.

Curious to see the Palace one last time, his spirit ventured through the corridors. He looked at the Palace's riches and decided they were frivolous and over extravagant, even vulgar; he never liked the paintings and sculpture his servants chose for him; they had no taste whatsoever, he decided. He moved into the kitchens and looked at the kitchen staff busy working on a feast. The food was rich and succulent, but he felt disgust for the opulence. He visited the wine cellars where there were rows upon row of the most expensive drinks available; all he had wanted was water and this seemed more precious than these extravagant processed fluids. What had been the point of them? Finally he came to the entrance halls; ornately decorated, the space they occupied would have provided shelter for a thousand of his subjects.

There was a commotion at the doorway at that moment, and a hurried group of concerned serving people fussed around the door. A stretcher was being rushed through the door and a doctor was being called. On the stretcher was a bloodied beaten body, its face unrecognisable, and in its hand it clutched tightly a handful of colourful gemstones. They fell from the hand as it was rushed along the corridor and scattered noisily along the floor, some falling into a drainage grille, thoroughly unseen and wasted.

Norman looked aghast at the scene and wondered who this poor unfortunate victim could be. And then at last as he surveyed the body, he noticed the shoes and around the blooded neck of the near corpse was his talisman.

Here was the new King Norman, who would wake from death hailed as an absent hero. He would be different, but then he had just survived a near death experience, and they would forgive him for that.

And, after all, everyone loved good old reliable safe King Norman."

"That's it, the end," he said, as he saw Finn looking with anticipation, as if for a punch line.

"And, is there some moral, then?" asked Finn.

"I don't really know," said Dara, now thinking on his feet. "But I think it's along the lines of be careful what you wish for, or just stay at home, if you can." Finn pondered long and hard on the meaning of this story, thinking there was a vague resonance with something in his own life, but he just couldn't think what, just then. Feeling he had to respond with a story of his own, Finn wracked his brains but the best he could do was to recount the plot of 'The Lion, the Witch, and the Wardrobe' only because he thought it had resonance in this land. Otherwise, it would have been an episode of Star Trek. Dara listened in rapture to the tale, even though Finn rushed through it, paraphrasing all the way.

"Oh well, if we are to cross this desert we'd better conserve some of this water," said Finn as he finally got to his feet. " We don't know how long we might be here, and this map is useless. It doesn't give you any idea whatsoever of distances. It full of lovely pictures, but what use are they to us. We need information."

"Well you aren't going to get it there," said Dara, cynically confirming his suspicions. "Which way then?"

"East, or whatever you call it here." Finn pointed in the right direction

"West," said Dara indistinctly as he chewed on some bread husk he had salvaged. "Your map's upside down," he laughed.

"What do you mean? If the battle field is there and we have travelled from there to here," he pointed at the two locations" …then it has to be East."

"No, the writing's upside down. We…are here," indicated Dara, pointedly and smugly.

"So, West it is, and we seem to have further, but then who knows?"

At that point, from out of the shadows a small man wearing monks robes passed by, hurriedly. His face was obscured, but a long gnarly finger stretched out and tapped on the map. He did not appear even to look in the direction of the confabulated brothers.

"West," he said in a husky, troubled voice, " …to the Barbarian's Gates, then follow your instincts." He had a superior air, and was sneering. As he passed by, he said, "You boys need all the help you can get…" Then he melted into the landscape. Open jawed, for they had not been in the slightest aware of him approaching, and this could have been fatal, Finn reminded Dara, as they watched him disappear.

They set off in the direction of the setting sun, which Finn realised should have given him some clues. Darkness fell like a soft velvet blanket and it was soon pitch black. The sky was moonless tonight, which was a strange occurrence in a sky with two, normally.

The horses were getting restless and obviously did not like the lack of vision, but Finn wanted them to press forward; he was severely impatient and frustrated with their lack of progress, now. But soon, the horses decided for them and they simply would not go any further, so Finn determined at last it was time to camp up for the night. It was so dark they could not see their feet in front of them, so instead of searching for firewood, they used their packs to rest their heads upon, covered themselves in blankets, and went straight to sleep. It had been a particularly long tiring day and both were asleep immediately.

Dawn seemed to come in the blink of an eye. Finn woke in the startling bright morning light, and rubbed his eyes in disbelief at the sight that greeted him. He woke Dara quickly and shook him into life.

"Don't make any sudden moves," he said, pushing back carefully and slowly with his heels, and Dara followed suit without any further convincing.

At their feet was a deep, deep, chasm, the sheer walls of a mile deep canyon, a fissure in the ground so deep they could not really see the bottom of it. The other wall of the canyon was only a matter of 100 metres across from them. It could have been 100 miles for all the comfort that brought. Looking over they saw birds circle like vultures far down below, and assumed that the bones of less fortunate travellers might be down there already. The birds mocked them, and seemed to be waiting for them.

"One more step and…" Finn didn't need to finish this sentence. "How did that happen? How did we not see it? Why isn't it on the map?"

Dara was too shaken to respond to the barrage of questions, and simply grunted. The horses were some distance from the void, and Finn was sure they had a haughty look on their impassive faces, like they were saying, "Told you so." But, these horses had just saved their lives, Finn reminded himself.

Once collected they picked up their things added them to the rolls on the saddles and contemplated the void before them, and how to get across it. They first set off along the lip of the canyon carefully tracing the edge, hoping it wouldn't crumble under them. Vertigo wasn't something Finn had thought about, before, particularly seated for the greater part of his recent life. Now his every thought was concentrated on it. He realised that they might walk on for hours like this. How to get across?

"What we need is a bridge, but there isn't the slightest chance of that here," he said out loud to whoever might hear, other than Dara.

As if to emphasise it, he shouted it across the canyon. "Where's the bridge, then?" The echo came back, quieter with each wave.

He sat down, now miserable, sulking like the teenager he was and how he had forgotten to in recent weeks. He picked at his tunic, unravelling the threads of the coat of arms emblazoned on his tunic chest. Dara looked down at him from the horse he had since mounted.

"We have got to keep going, Finn. It's hot and we haven't enough water with us. We've got to keep moving"

"But this is no use. This canyon isn't even on the map so we don't know where we are heading." He was now angry and frustrated.

"What's that there," said Dara, pointing at an almost imperceptible activity on the ground ahead. Finn looked up, now interested. He could see the movement, and they both headed over to look.

"It's only an ants nest," Finn said in final realisation, his hopes of something mystical dashed. But the ants were more interesting than the empty void or the potential journey along the canyon, so they stopped to watch them busily working and gathering what scraps of food they could.

It soon became clear they were not gathering but had some greater strategy in their collective mind. From one or two scurrying insects the colony grew in number on the ground. Soon there were thousands of ants. This was getting a bit freaky for Finn, who wasn't totally comfortable with insect life at the best of times. He backed off a little. The ants were not interested in Finn, however, and busily worked together forming a pathway of shimmering black towards the edge of the canyon. Thousands became millions soon and as they clambered over each other they formed a knotted solid mass. Others scurried over the mass and soon they cantilevered out over the canyon edge.

"Look Finn," said Dara. " There's your bridge!"

It was true. The ants were forming a pathway right out over the canyon; billions of them forming a single monolithic mass, arching out across the void. They could see the same thing on the other side of the canyon. Finn, awestruck, wondered exactly how many it took, and how it might be happening. Whilst it took hours to build, it was absolutely fascinating to watch and as they finished it dawned on Finn that they would have to put their trust in these mindless, collective creatures, to step out into the unknown and cross the void. It would simply be bad manners not to.

When completed the arched bridge was black as night and the shimmering movement finally stopped. The bridge had the appearance of the most elegant and slight structure that Finn had ever seen, and it looked impossibly fragile. It was as if noise had stopped too, for an imperceptible rustling noise had been pervasive since the ants had started toiling. Only when it was gone was it obvious. Just like the racket from Finn's PC in his old home, in another time, another place, now largely forgotten. They hesitated for an instant and then each took that first tentative step onto the ants.

Finn expected the structure to dissolve into nothingness as soon as they were over the canyon. I have to trust my instinct, he thought, remembering the Monk's words. This didn't happen for nothing, he thought. Someone made this happen; someone orchestrated these tiny creatures to create something far beyond their intellect or experience. They had seemed driven, and he had to trust them. It did not, of course, cross his mind that he may have done this.

Gaining confidence, they crossed carefully. The bridge was only a couple of metres wide and with no guard rail there was no saving the wavering traveller. Finn stared straight ahead, tensely looking into the distance. The bridge held, and after five minutes of sheer terror he was across. As they looked back the bridge dissolved back into its millions of individual components, as if it had never existed, which was probably closer to the truth than Finn cared to admit to himself.

Relieved, they looked around for a place to rest, and for some water source and a babbling stream formed a small waterfall over the ledge. Dara filled their canteens, they each took a long draught and collapsed in laughter and relief. Two minutes later they were on their way again.

……

Far from here, and unknown to them, a plan was being hatched and Blue Moonstone was being leisurely tossed into an azure lake, hissing as it skimmed the surface. As the stone sank into the depths, The Guardian scowled at the still water and saw in its mirrored surface the desert landscape and the black bridge of ants.

Finn's yell of frustration had reached back through the distance, and it resonated with potent, untapped magic. The Guardian knew this feeling well. He had laughed at the naivety of the young Prince, unaware of the immense, untapped power he might have at his fingertips, and using it without conscious knowledge.

Well, he could teach him a thing or two, and knowing their next milestone on the journey to Finn's Father, he set a trap; one which had been waiting patiently at an ancient place The Guardian had visited once in his younger days, and was now coming to fruition.

16 *The Gateway.*

There it was, right in front of them, the Gateway they had been promised by the Monk. It stood in an open plain and comprised two sandstone pillars, translucent green in colour, and each pillar supported an equally massive timber door studded with blackened iron rivets. They looked uncannily similar to the doors to the Castle, and Finn surmised they had the same designer. Thinking back to his old life, when he read fantasy novels, or thought about craftsmen building Castles, he hadn't even considered that some design might have gone into these structures. It was as thought they just grew, or that some bloke had an image of how it might look in his head and directed the workers to create this image, more like art than science.

But they must have had some design. He remembered, though, reading that mediaeval cathedrals were built, then collapsed and were rebuilt and collapsed again, and again, until in the end they got it right and the building stayed upright. Look at the Leaning Tower of Pisa. No amount of design could have created that.

The fact that the Gates resembled the Castle doors both reassured and worried him in equal measure. What if The Guardian had some influence here. What if they were being watched from a distance? This was tricky, dangerous and potentially fatal, but they had to go on. Somehow the existence of freedom in the Homeland, and beyond, depended entirely on his naïve head and shoulders.

The other odd thing about the gates was of course that they stood entirely on their own. There seemed to be nothing stopping you from just ducking around the sides. It was as if an enormous wall once existed, of which there was no trace left. But the imposing size of the gates implied some ominous threat if you followed that foolish course of action, and that you simply had to go through them. How, was a different matter.

As they approached they could feel the hum of power from the Gates, and the horses reared up in fear, almost throwing their riders. Both Finn and Dara decided at once that walking was a better idea, and they dismounted. Gently coaxing and leading the horses, they approached the Gates and they seemed to grow larger and more imposing as they got nearer. The reason for this was that they were indeed getting larger and more imposing, and their initial perspective had been distorted by the immense dimensions of the Gates and the immeasurable empty plain on which they impressively and impassively stood.

"Jeez, this is going to be impossible," said Finn defeatedly as they arrived at the face of the Gates.

"I wasn't going to say that, in case you jumped down my throat," replied his brother.

"We have to think of some strategy," said Finn. " If this was a Playstation game or on a Wii then there would be a specific code to follow, we just have to find it." He thought dreamily of how he had been thankful his hands still worked, even if his legs hadn't.

Dara looked at him vacantly, concerned by this apparent attack of gibberish, just when some serious thought and action was required.

Dara had a strategy already, and it involved a large rock. He picked it up and threw it at the Gate. To his amazement, it didn't quite reach the Gate, but stayed suspended in mid air some six inches from the timber face, crackling with energy and light. Then it exploded into a million fragments in a controlled but slow motion. They both ducked out of the way of the fragments, but somehow they were untouched by any of them, and the pieces disappeared as though vapour.

"Well, let that be a lesson," said Dara smugly, as though he was under the impression this was Finn's first line of attack.

"Try that again." He said. "…But not at the gate, try the space next to the pillar." This time the rock died a more spectacular, fiery death, and Finn though carefully about how he had first thought this was just a double bluff and you could just walk round the Gates, and was thankful he hadn't just tried.

"How far d'you think it stretches, I mean could we walk along it a bit and get through?"

Dara shrugged his shoulders and basically said, "Hhhnnh?"

They sat for some hours trying to think of how to deal with this insurmountable problem. After some time they were both hungry and each ate some fruit. The succulent juicy fruits were delicious and they savoured each mouthful, as each was a rare treat now, with no idea of how long they needed to conserve supplies. Dara had carelessly thrown away an apple core, and it bounced near to the base of the Gate. Although they hadn't noticed immediately, the fact that the core didn't explode or burst into flames soon became of great interest. It was close to the Gate but they couldn't risk stretching over to get it.

Out from nowhere, a tiny mouse like creature with a long snout darted out, straight into the Gate and grabbed the core, stuffing it in a pocket and ran off with its prize. It didn't explode either. What could this mean?

Finn took a leap of faith and announced that the Gate must be able to detect intent. If you planned an incursion on it or to damage it in some way, it would defend itself, if you didn't then it didn't.

"I'm going to try something," he said, with his fingers crossed, and he strode over to it hand in a fist, and simply knocked. Nothing happened, he sighed with relief; he didn't explode, start floating in mid air, or dissolve.

And then something did happen. Twenty metres away in the foot of the Gate a small door opened, and a head poked out. Only a head. It appeared unattached to any other appendage of body.

"What do you want?" asked the owner of the head, which was bald and shining, with knobbly ridges on both sides above pointed ears.

"Eh, can we come in?" he said. "I'm looking for my Father"

"Ohh, poor lost boys," said the head. "Come on through, I do like to help people."

"What about our horses? They could never get through that tiny door," Dara shouted over.

"You children know nothing these days," said the head, exasperated. "Just drag them over, they'll pass through."

Finn and Dara looked at each other, packed up their things and walked their horses to the Gate. The horses looked enormous next to the little door, but Finn bent down to pass through anyway. Next thing he knew he was through the other side, and he pulled on the reins. Whilst the door didn't grow, or his horse shrink, something weird happened, and the horse passed through easily. Dara followed and the same thing happened. Finn watched intently, but could not fathom how it had worked.

The head said, "Told you, but would you believe me…?" and then the door slammed shut, and the hum disappeared and the Gates vanished in a swoosh of sound, sucked into an oblivion beyond their imagination.

And then they were in a wide open landscape, with nothing ahead of them and nothing behind them. The sun was beating down and it was getting hotter all the while. Finn could hear his own heart beating. The desert in front of them was barren and lifeless; a void. There was no cloud in the sky and the sun was at a high point. It blinded them with both its intensity and its heat and they squinted at the bright, yellow whiteness, which blotted out any other possible feature. He was panicked now, but he knew that this could not be real. It had to be illusion, once again. But what was the illusion hiding. What was actually there? How could he find out?

The obvious thing was to accept the illusion and walk on as they had done at the chasm. It struck him that this was the opposite of that illusion. If that was true then he had to tread carefully. The darkness that time had hidden something illusory that had threatened them; their own fear made physical. The threat of the fall was worse than the actuality. The threat had been empty. Like everything here, he thought. In this place, though, there was nothing. Flat earth. He thought immediately of the music from the first banquet, the night he arrived. The formless void of the magical musical instruments that had filled his head with …nothing. He had ventured in rapture into a vast empty space, and the sound had invited him in and he had accepted the invitation. And, now, here he was in real nothingness, emptiness, and he knew it was inside his head. That didn't stop it being disturbing. He shook his head as if this would change things. But it didn't. He thought of the music and tried to turn it off. But it didn't change anything. He closed his eyes, but the blistering heat burned ever harder. No shade, no trees, no shelter. Finally he surrendered to the illusion.

"Let's go, Dara," he said softly." But watch your step"

The words had hardly left his lips when right in front of him Dara disappeared into the sand. Finn screamed out his name, watching helplessly as the cone of sand opened up in front of him as if he were trapped inside an egg timer in a steaming hot bright kitchen. Trapped in a globe, watched from outside.

He couldn't catch Dara and he disappeared, horse and all, into the whirlpool of sand ahead of him. He screamed and cried out loud but he couldn't make a sound. He reached out, stretching as far as he could, in vain. The air was being sucked out of the globe; the glass case wouldn't let sound out. He was silent, and in his silent scream, it struck him, again.

Follow your instincts.

Horse reins in hand he marched towards the swirling sand pool and slipped into it. There was no stopping him, nothing to hold onto and soon he and horse and everything around was tumbling and falling round and round, sucked into the void of sand like a bubble of soap twisting into an open plug hole. Sand was drowning him, entering his mouth and ears and nose and he couldn't breathe. This time it wasn't illusion, he was thinking. It's real! And it must be the end…

And he fell further than he could imagine. Lights flashed around him as his mind filled the blanks in the sensory deprivation in which he now found himself. He was twisting and turning and falling. Blue, then green, then bright sunlight blinding him. The flashes came thick and fast and the pounding noise in his head was excruciating. Occasionally he thought he saw Dara twisting past him, but then he thought it was illusion. Then he hit soft earth with a jolt, and passed out, not for the first time.

17 *Woodentops*

Birds twittered in the trees, which were…. outside. Sun and heat streamed in through an open window with billowing friendly curtains. It was directly in his face and he was blinded. There was a quiet scuffling around him, and a silent concern. He lay in a comfortable if hard bed, swaddled in blankets, cosily too warm, but the soporific feeling was irresistible. He felt as though he was swimming in silky, warmed milk.

"Who, exactly, is it?" he heard a voice say, through the haze.

"Well, we're not really sure," said another in hushed tones. " But it seemed to be hurt, so what else could I do? I had to bring it here."

"You could just have…." The sentence wasn't, thankfully, finished.

In the bright white sunlight Finn squinted again, and could make out two figures across the room. He couldn't tell who they were, or what, but they seemed both close up and, at the same time, far away. Giants perhaps?

"Look, it's just moved. Isn't it lovely? I haven't seen one like this before. Look at the hair."

"And you say it just appeared from nowhere?"

"Fell out of the sky, I think. It was behind me so I can't really tell. Just heard a noise. It wasn't there one minute, then it was…."

"Where did it come from then?"

"Who knows?"

Finn drifted off again and dreamt of his fall through space. Or rather he dreamt of being in a bright red London Routemaster bus falling over Beachy Head in England. The bus trundled on over the 700 feet high cliffs. The conductor was there, smiling. Old and smiling. The same old man again. But the strangest thing was Finn wasn't scared. He just sat on the front seat of the top deck and marvelled at the trip, accepting it as though this was a Sunday trip to the zoo. Straight down. But he didn't land, so he must be OK....

As he woke again, a hand was soothingly wiping his brow, which was fevered in an old fashioned way. It was a large hand, with gnarled old fingers the texture of tree trunks. He didn't care much that it was an ugly hand; it was like his mother when he was a little child. He had the flu' and she was there to stop him worrying. Glucose drink, in little bottles, yellow and tasty.

His eyes came into focus, and he realized this was, basically, a tree. Deceptively huge and brown and leafy, but also, unbelievably, it was human formed, too. He couldn't quite grasp its true form, but at that moment he didn't really care. Thoroughly convinced he was still in a dream, he allowed the insanity of this situation wash over him. Trees talking, he thought lazily.

After a day or so he woke up, properly. He was in the bed, the comfortable but hard bed, wrapped in blankets, the taste of sweet tea on his lips stopping the dehydration but not letting him waste energy trying to eat solids. Moist lips. That was good. It was a cool evening now and he peeled off the blankets and tried to stand. He couldn't move his legs, he couldn't feel them either and this brought back the helpless feeling of the wheelchair days. Panicked, he let out a little involuntary squeal. All the time they haven't worked, he thought.

There was a scurrying sound, and he realised he wasn't quite dreaming. The tree person did exist. It came rushing in to the room, with a dishcloth in its… hands, obviously drying some dishes or carrying out some other mundane task that he didn't expect any fantastic creature might ever contemplate. Again he couldn't really explain it. His perception was of trees, but also of person. In confusion he just accepted it.

"You're awake, little thing," it said.

Finn was aware that he had been there for some time, and so far no harm had come to him. In fact, just the opposite, so let's take a chance, he thought.

He murmured some incoherent grunt. Wait a minute, he thought internally. I can understand myself when I think, but when I talk, it's …rubbish…. but I can talk to the trees?

Soup was hurriedly brought to his bedside, and he thankfully gulped it down, although the spoon was a bit on the big side. More grunting followed.

"Yes you've been very unwell, for a long, long time," said the tree-woman, understanding him. (She was too helpful, and nice, to be a man he had decided; a bit like a mum, he thought)

"You seem to have hurt your legs," said the friendly voice. "We've splinted them up. You won't feel anything though because we've given you some …medicine." Finn was extremely relieved by this news, but still wanted reassurance.

"Yessss, don't worry about it. You will soon be back on your tiny legs. Well, what happened to you then?" The other tree arrived to listen to the conversation and soon Finn was recounting his saga. It was an internal conversation with himself, but they listened seemingly enthralled by the adventure.

"So you, let me see, are on a quest?" said Tree One, a bit too patronisingly for Finn's liking. "And you're detained here now. So what is happening back home? And what about your brother?"

Finn had somehow forgotten about following Dara into the quicksand. Again the panic rose in his chest and he felt the need to get out there and find Dara. But that wasn't going to happen. He still couldn't walk, even if he wanted to.

"I've got to get away from here," Finn said out loud finally and apologetically, for these people were so kind and helpful, but he needed to get going. Time was of the essence.

"You can't leave," the tree said. "What would we do without you, now?"

Finn gulped. "Trapped again," he thought. "How do I get out of this one?" Alone and scared he decided to take his time and wait for opportunity to knock.

A whole week passed, slowly. Still no sign of Dara. Still no rescue, but lots of soup and care and rest. He could feel the strength in his legs coming back, and thought that this at least was a blessing. They weren't irreparably damaged this time. And his own voice began to sound normal to him, now.

The tree people were nicer than nine-pence, but he was beginning to feel totally trapped. He told them earnestly that he wanted to go, but they would hear nothing of it.

"You have only just arrived," they said clingingly. Over the endless, tedious time he only had his thoughts to help him. Not only did time stretch out, but there was nothing, absolutely nothing, to fill it. He was beginning to understand how a tree might actually feel, its long interminably slow life stretching out before it with nothing to do but stay where you were and grow. And with that blinding flash of realisation, he knew he would never get out of this prison.

These were trees, this was what they knew. They didn't necessarily mean any harm, but to them only seconds must have passed since his arrival. And they planned to keep him here as some kind of surrogate sapling. True they looked after him and seemed genuinely concerned for his welfare. But he wasn't a tree. How to escape? They didn't seem to sleep so he couldn't just get out by running away. They would hear him and make chase. He couldn't persuade them to let him go, they seemed so lonely.

Mulling over his predicament he noticed his bag was still with him, and he leaned over, picked it carefully and quietly up and rummaged around in it. The first thing he came across was a knife, the sharp point of which stuck in his hand painfully. Then there was an apple, then the sheathed skean dubh. Perhaps he could brandish this at them, but it would just stick into them and then be worse than useless. He needed something that was frightening enough to scare them, but wouldn't really harm them. What could he use?

Delving further, he felt a shiny stainless steel casing and wondered what this was. It turned out to be a Zippo lighter, the very same as the one his Dad used when they went camping. It had been his Grandad's during the war and he had scraped his initials on it in a fit of boredom, no doubt in between the hell of battle. (Finn's 20th Century Grandad, it transpired had never got out of Catterick Barracks where he worked in the catering corps, and he had used the lighter for no other war faring purpose than lighting the gas hob, to cook the spuds. But his long tales of derring-do in the North Africa and the Middle East with Monty had convinced the family he had been in more danger than he actually saw. Finn, of course, knew nothing of this. Like his Great Uncle who had been mauled by a lion. Grandad informed the family this had been when his Brother, John, had been exploring the upper delta of the Nile. No one bothered to check if there were lions this far up in Africa, but the scars and the tale corresponded nicely, so everyone believed to his dying day.

The truth came out, that the circus had come to town, and Great Uncle John had ventured a bit too close to the lion cage at the after circus zoo…and was mauled for his nosiness. Threepence not so well spent, but a great story for the archives. It seemed there was a great deal of imagination in Finn's family.) It seemed odd to Finn that a 20th century lighter, complete with fuel unknown, normally, in these parts, would materialise in his bag, but he took the opportunity once it became evident. The thing about a Zippo lighter is the enormous flame it can produce, particularly indoors away from the elements. A light bulb flashed, metaphorically of course, above his head.

"Can I have some water please?" he yelled from his bed once his manoeuvres and strategy were in place. The Tree man and woman both came stumbling in; concerned their care was in distress.

"I need to get up," he said cunningly. " I need to get out of bed and get a drink"

They leant over to help him to his feet and then he struck! However, meaning only to brandish the flame around enough to scare them, his cuff got caught in the blanket and he dropped the fiery lighter. Horrified, he watched it fall into the folds and next thing the entire bed was ablaze.

This time he jumped out of the bed, but thinking quickly, reached in and grabbed the lighter up, closed it, and then tried to put out the flames with his hands, to no avail. The Tree people were screaming. He had been right. This was their worst nightmare, and he had brought it in, in spades, and unwittingly. He was ashamed, for they had been so pleasant, but also he needed to escape and he ran for the door shouting, "I'm sorry, I'm sorry. I didn't mean to do it. …S-s-sorry!"

18 *Escape*

Fleeing the Tree people and their burning house, he felt thoroughly depressed. They had been nothing but kind to him really, looked after him, and yet he was repaying the kindness in the most horrifying, horrible way. But they *had* wanted him trapped and he couldn't live as their pet forever. He reconciled his feelings, thus.

As he fled, running as fast as his recuperated legs could carry him, his breath was heavy and his chest heaving. Not only was the acrid smoke following him, but also, the wails of the Tree people were ringing in his ears long after he was out of sight of the flaming house. He vowed to repay them somehow, but just now he needed to get away. He needed to find his lost brother, and he needed to get back on track. Who knows what had happened in the time he had wasted here, slowly growing older. The one thing he did know was that his horse was safe and sound, since he had spotted it tied to a tree near the flaming house. He realised with dawning remorse he would have to return to the scene of his crime to steal back his horse under cover of darkness, and he hoped there would be no posse of trees looking for him, or waiting in ambush for his potential return.

He now had no idea where he was, when he was, and if he was. His only hope here was the map. The map had, fortunately turned back to normal and now revealed landscape, rolling hills, a long snaking river leading back into the Homeland where the Castle stood imposingly atop its hill, and mountains with a well defined path through to the sea. There at the end of the route was the Five Fathoms, distinctly shown. Bizarrely he noticed there was a large drawing pin drawn scratchily, as if by some five year old, onto the map, with an additional flapping sign attached. The legend, of course, stated 'YOU ARE HERE!' wherever here actually was.

He waited patiently behind a tree in a little snug mossy hollow, occasionally drifting off, until night fell and made his way back to the burnt house. His worst fears were realised when he got there as the two sad Tree people were still sitting aimlessly amongst the ruins of their house, gathering what remaining belongings had survived. They knew he was there and glowered in his direction.

"You had better take that beast and get on with your useless quest," one said. " You could have been happy with us, untroubled, we would have made sure you were safe."

They were two sad parents saying goodbye to their son as he left for a new life far away from them, knowing they would never get as much as a Christmas card again, unless he needed money that is.... Resignedly they walked out and led his horse to him.

"Don't like these big beasts, by the way."

When the reins were in his hands. Finn was awkward and speechless. He finally plucked up the courage and spoke up.

" I'm really, I mean, truly, sorry. I only meant to get away. I meant to scare you away so I could get out, it was an accident…." he blurted out hurriedly. The words trailed away into silence.

"Don't worry, we understand."

"Look, I can make it up to you, somehow I will. I just need to get on and find my Dad. It's so very important, everyone is relying on me. I am sure he will reward you and get you a new house or something…I'll come back…I promise."

There was silence.

"If you see my brother please send him this way," and he pulled out the map. It was still wrapped in a burgundy coloured velvet scroll, with the bright yellow thread of the family coat of arms sewn boldly across it. There was a different type of stunned silence when they saw the coat of arms.

"Why didn't you say sooner, who your family are? We could have saved a lot of time. Look, in these parts you get a lot of people on quests. Every traveller seems to have some cock and bull story about hidden treasure or rings and princesses. If we knew this time we had a real Prince in our house, then.....Well, we are absolutely honoured that you chose our house to burn down., and not our bad tempered neighbours over there. They would have eaten you by the way. Now," he paused to think. "Business....We need to get you going. You're very late for a very important appointment it seems, there is no time to spare. You must forgive us for detaining you."

"We can help, you know," he said as he held out his knotty palm flat in front of his mouth and blew through a pile of feather light dandelion clock seeds on it. A misty and sparkling light emanated from his hand and grew, the cloud spreading off towards the embedded trees of the forest. Soon there was a wind whistling through the leaves and the branches swung wildly and happily. Like a wave the breeze headed off into the distance, leaves whispering and blowing as the wave traversed the forest.

"This wind is your friend," he finally said, " ...and all the trees will know you. They will help when it is needed most." He handed some of the seeds to Finn, in a small purse.

"Guard these with your life. They are valuable and may save you when the time comes. You can talk to the trees through them. Just blow a handful and think your wish and they will respond."

"I knew your Father, you see. And I know only he can bring safety and freedom back to our joined lands. I fought beside him. Before he was deposed, of course. He is a great man, a great warrior, and a great friend to nature. We need him now…before all is lost. You really should have said his name earlier," the Tree man said tersely and disapprovingly. He smiled, though, and indicated a disturbance in the distance, through the darkness.

"Ah, here comes help!"

A rider was approaching as if driven by the very wind itself. High up on a massive steed, the warrior looked impressive and formidable. Wearing a tailored, fine fitting armoured suit, with a purple cloak of silk flowing in the backdraft caused by his speed, and a black helmet which covered all his features, with a cowl behind his neck to prevent blows from behind, the warrior flew through the forest tracks, skilfully avoiding the low slung branches with deft weaving and bobbing.

The horse was armoured too, and the saddle was equipped with a variety of swords and other strange looking weapons. An array of what looked to Finn like hand grenades was strung along a bandolier around the horse's girth. The beast itself was the most magnificent creature Finn had seen since arriving in the Homelands; it snorted and whinnied and had a fearsome presence. Shiny and black under its thin armour, steam exuded from its muscular torso as it ran.

Approaching, his speed and urgency quickened further as the devastation of the fire became evident. As the Warrior drew to a stop right beside them, Finn marvelled at the mind-blowing sight, the very size of the horse and its rider towering above them. He also gawped at the enormous sword that had been hurriedly drawn as the unknown warrior surveyed the scene.

Presently a voice, deep and booming within the confines of the helmet, yet strangely soft, with a feminine touch, said, "What is it Rotwangle? What's happened here? Did The Guardian do this? I'm sorry, I came as fast as I could."

Trying to avoid the inevitable fuss and potential for misunderstanding Rotwangle said quickly, "Many thanks for your prompt arrival. Ignore the house. That can be fixed! We have an emergency, here. This young man is on an urgent quest and needs escorting beyond the mountains to the sea. He is alone. Can you help him, as a favour to your old, old friend? Oh, and do you see who this is?"

The helmeted face looked from the smoking ruins down onto the face of the relatively diminutive Finn from on high, shaking from side to side.

"This is none other than Finn McGarrigle, the Lord High Protector of the Homelands, son of Evan McGarrigle, King of the Homelands and the seven counties beyond. Just get off the horse and pay some respects. This young man is our Saviour; our best hope for freedom, for a normal life…"

The rider dismounted as though an order had come from heaven and a thunderbolt was awaiting disobedience. The rider was tall, even knelt before Finn grasping a sword for support in a cross in front of him, hands clasped on the hilt, eyes downward cast.

"You must forgive me for not recognising you, Sire," said the now tremulous voice in the helmet. The rider stood and turned, fumbling with the straps awkwardly in gloved hands as though all assertiveness had dropped away. Standing now, in temper and frustration the gloves were soon dropped to the ground. The helmet came off slowly to reveal something Finn had not expected. A woman.

She shook her head as the helmet was removed and long platinum hair flowed from it, whipping from side to side covering her face for an instant, revealing it the next. Finn looked intently into the face; her fiery, alive green eyes, the elegant, high cheekbones, and her fine pointed chin. His eyebrows raised in surprise.

"Finn McGarrigle, Lord High Protector and all that," said Rotwangle, bowing with a flourish; "Meet Her Most Magnificent Highness; Ségolène Rambeaut, Warrior Princess from Vieux Orleans, beyond the Emerald Ocean. Deliverer of Souls, Protector of the Seal of Rémy, Only Living Holder of the Ancient Order of Merlin, Destroyer of the Legendary Vardrigal ….And all the rest."

19 *The Mountain Pass*

Finally gathering their provisions and waving their goodbyes to Rotwangle and his wife, Gwalchmai, Finn and Ségolène soon set a course on their respective horses and headed out of the forest in the direction of the mountains. As they travelled and climbed, the weather changed and almost instantly it was noticeable that the temperature had dramatically dropped. Finn wrapped his protective cloak around himself, felt the warmth, and thought about his brother. There seemed nothing he could do, so resignedly, they continued on their way.

Snow was soon falling and the climb became steeper. The horses remained sure-footed and as they climbed higher steam could be seen blowing from their round open nostrils. They would whinny resentfully every so often, complaining about their lot, but pressed on regardless. The trees were sparser here and had changed from the exuberant green deciduous trees of the valley floor to spiny, sharp-needled pine trees, with little carpets of snow and ice weighing down their branches. Finn was certain he could hear them whispering to him guiding him on, as if Rotwangle had passed his message through these trees to protect him on his journey. They seemed comforting, assuring him they would contain the snow and save him from harm and the worst excesses of the cold.

As night fell and they decided they had to camp up, a clearing appeared before them, with a scattered pile of dropped branches almost inviting a fire to be made. Once set, the flames glowed and danced merrily, and perceptibly the density of the surrounding trees seemed to increase, as if to stop any forest beast, or enemy fighter from entering their circle of safety. In the glow of the fire, they chatted about Finn's situation and they feasted on the luscious fruits they had found scattered randomly amongst the branches.

"So, you are telling me that you haven't always been here, or you have always been here and you are suffering from some delusion that you were somewhere else; somewhere which was totally real to you. Or, you are suffering some delusion and you aren't here at all?" Ségolène ran through the possibilities, out loud.

"Well if you aren't here, then neither am I. Or, perhaps you are a figment of my imagination!"

"Look it hurts my head to think about it in any way whatsoever," said Finn. " I don't know which is right. I've been having dreams here where I am back in my old life, but it melds in with this one. I don't know what's reality any more."

"It's simple, really. Reality is only what you experience. If you are here, you are here. If you are in the land of metal and noise you describe, that's the reality. If things appear from nowhere and try to eat you, that's reality and you have to deal with it right there and then. If The Guardian is trying to destroy you, then he is. It's that simple. That's how to think," Ségolène said pragmatically, looking upwards at the stars through the clearing.

As they sat in the pendulous silence that followed her pronouncement, the message dawned on Finn that it did not matter what reality was, he had to live here for now and get on with life. And if he was still back in the 21st Century, he would wake some time and he now knew he could accept his lot. He had to be more optimistic. There was trouble and strife everywhere, and his life simply wasn't that bad. He was suddenly disgusted with his previous behaviour. These days (and he laughed to himself at the phrase, wondering exactly what that now meant) you could do anything. Having difficulty walking was no barrier to a successful life. Look at Stephen Hawking, he thought. Look at all those people who just get on with their life, without complaint, without the depression, without misery. Sure everyone gets a bit down now and again, but they pull through. No one liked me because I was a misery, not because of the wheelchair. I didn't give them the chance.

His musing and the silence was broken by a scurrying, scratching sound that emanated from beyond the protective barrier of the trees. Ségolène raised a finger to her mouth. Someone, or something, was there trying to get through to them. It was like a million tiny fingernails scratching at the tree trunks.

The noise was not constant but came in fits and starts as if it were moving away and trying to find a new bolt hold, some weakness in the ring of trees that it could exploit. An eternity seemed to pass and they listened in the darkness, not totally without fear, but both of them secure in the knowledge the trees would protect them. There was a whistling sound and the wind grew in force outwith the centre of safety. Branches began to bend and shake, whisking back and forward as far as their elasticity would allow. Each stroke was answered with a whiplash return of the branch to its original position, and the whole mass of trees was acting as one, creating a pattern. Soon the treetops were bending down and whipping back into position, and the noise created overwhelmed the scratching sounds.

A moaning soon replaced the scratching and in a whiplash motion the tree on what would be the north face of the circle erupted in an explosive outburst, bending and picking up the unseen assailant and throwing it with a force so strong the sound of its rough landing was not heard for several minutes. It sounded massive, but still they had no idea of what it could have been. However, taking advantage of the sudden break in the tree circle the gap was filled with a million scurrying spiders, rushing in as a river of black, and homing in on the hapless duo in the centre of the circle of fear.

Again the trees recovered their calm, and both Ségolène and Finn were lifted high by the bending tree tops, straight out of the way of the massing spiders, and up into the tree tops. Finn could see their horses and belongings far below in danger of attack by the spiders, but again the trees reacted and the creatures and individual belongings were lifted to a height of safety. The mindless mass of spiders continued to congregate in the centre of the circle finding only the fire, burning brightly.

At that moment the tree tops buckled again and dipping into the centre of the flames, pulled the burning embers in a controlled fashion from the centre of the circle, engulfing the spiders as the ring of fire made its way from centre to edge. The screams of the spiders as they burned could be heard distinctly at the tops of the trees and Finn closed his eyes and hoped for it to end. He had never in his lifetime of squashing these creatures ever given them thought, and these seemed more real than any he had killed before. Soon there was silence again and the trees lowered them gently back into the circle, the fire having been restored as though never disturbed, and they were left in peace to continue their conversation.

"Want a game of cards?" asked Finn, trying both to return to normality and ascertain if Ségolène could work out the cards he had looked at all those days ago. The pressure and strain made him think about Dara, again and he shuddered visibly. Ségolène wrapped a tense arm around him and said some soothing words. He felt better immediately with a protector. He was not alone, but was Dara? Who was there to protect him from harm?

"I am sure he will turn up. You were safe after all. Perhaps some other Tree family has him. We can find out on our way back…."

Finn wasn't totally impressed with this. But what else could he do? His journey was too important to risk taking any more time. What might have happened in the Homelands in his absence?

He slept fitfully that night, dreaming of the dragons and hobgoblins, spiders and dwarves of his fantasy fiction at home. This had been his only remaining pastime where he could lose himself and be whole again. He had collected and read all the books; he watched all the fantasy films he could, and immersed himself in the fiction. Only now, these things seemed much more real than anything he had read in the books. The whole night, the whole land, was filled with fantasy.

A blistering white sun awoke him, and he saw that Ségolène was already up and about cooking some small beast, which she had obviously just killed, on a stick in the fire. She held up the stick invitingly offering it to her ward, with eyebrows raised in suggestion. Finn grimaced at the thought and shook his head.

"Not really MacDonalds is it?" he said. Ségolène looked at him not quite understanding.

They cleared up and looked at the map. It showed the next stage of the journey was through a mountain pass, followed by a nice flat plain down to the Ocean, and on to their destination. Nothing could be simpler. The horses laden, they set off, discussing trivia on the way. Finn tried to explain how a CD player worked, and television, but these were just beyond his companion. On the other hand, the magical powers of a wizard's crook were beyond Finn's normal experience too, so they swapped technologies all the way.

Ségolène embellished her chatter with tales of incredible bravery, or foolhardiness, dependant upon your outlook, of how she vanquished various violent magical creatures like the Vardrigal, or the evil Red Knight, who was eight feet three tall, and rode a horse with flaming armour. She had drowned him, quenching the flames with a charmed bucket filled with an endless supply of magical water. She swore as she recounted how this useful tool was lost in a hurried retreat through the Farmountains, running away from an army of The Guardian's Trolls. It should be simple to locate, for it had created a meandering new river heading to the Emerald Ocean, having presumably been tipped on its side in its fall.

Soon the trail began to rise higher and they were heading into Mountains. Ségolène informed him that the New River was only some hundred miles north of this location. Because of its provenance, it had magical healing properties and anyone bathing in it would have their various ills and pains treated. There were myths of it bestowing the ultimate property of endless youth, if you drank enough of it. She firmly did not believe this, but was open to persuasion.

The trail became rougher and Ségolène became silent, carefully scanning the skyline. She did not trust the environment they now found themselves in, as trees and escarpments restricted sightlines. There were beasts in these mountains that could kill them easily, even accidentally, such as bears, not to mention the ever-present threat of the enemy, whoever they may be. Every slight noise, a breaking twig, an eagle launching itself from the treetops, the hoot of an owl, made her significantly more tense and alert. Finn was largely unaware of the exact threat, but knew he could rely on her to think for him. There were times to delegate, and this was obviously one of them.

In silence they progressed. The trail was levelling, and above them high cliffs enclosed them. The cliff face was made of large rough hewn blocks of rock, held together by an impossibly weak looking sandy mortar, and to Finn the rocks looked as though they might collapse in on the pass at any moment. Added to this was the disconcerting feeling that the blocks made faces in the rocks; strong silent faces of the ancient peoples who had travelled this pass in time immemorial. They all looked immensely sad, as if a terrible fate had trapped them in the rock faces, or they had witnessed too many atrocities. Ségolène became aware of the awestruck look on Finn's face and correctly surmised what was on his mind.

"You are right Finn, these are the faces of the ancient tribesmen who lived her, long before you or I or our kind walked these lands. They are gone now, lost in the mists of time. They guard the pass with their stony silent impassive faces. But they have no power; they can only assimilate the tales, watch passively what happens here and perhaps in some distant future they will act. Who can tell? We need not fear them. They are our friends."

This was the most dangerous part of the journey and the level of fear was increasing as they moved through it. Ségolène knew something was wrong and again she placed her finger to her lips indicating '*shhh*' to Finn and pointed up to the cliff tops. Above the faces, there was a scrabbling noise and some debris fell from the cliff ledge onto them. Nothing serious, just dust and small branches. But what could be causing this?

Then all at once, all hell broke loose. High above them, unseen, unknown assailants had grouped together and began to make whooping sounds, screams of rage and the screeching noises of banshees howling. It was as if an army of monkeys and parrots and ravens had amassed waiting for them and Finn had stolen the firstborn of each.

Soon, rocks were raining down, and the horses bolted. This was helpful but the rocks just bounded after them, the screams following along the cliff top. Soon a liquid was pouring down. They decided not to wait to find out what it was or what it might do to them. They were dive-bombed by enormous birds carrying stones that pelted them, painfully. Finn drew his cloak over his head to protect himself, wondering at the same time how the flimsy material could help, but to his surprise it seemed to become solid, metallic and protective. The stones simply rebounded clanging noisily off the surface of the cloak.

The end of the pass was in view and the descent to safety. They flew like the wind towards it, but before they reached it, a smaller group appeared on horseback in the exit, armed to the teeth, dressed in the imperial colours of the Homeland. Behind them a small infantry of Troll like people appeared.

Finn and Ségolène drew to an immediate halt jumping from their horses. Ségolène ran towards Finn and wrapped her arms round him to protect him. He knew instinctively to bring the cloak round their forms for immediate protection. However, they were completely trapped.

Arrows rained down on them, but protected within the safety of the shelter they were all right. Under the cloak they both rapidly thought of ways to get out of the fix. Finn knew the cloak would provide protection, but for how long, and their foe was approaching. They would be captured if they did not take some action there and then.

Finn was soon to discover that Ségolène was not referred to as a Warrior Princess for nothing. In an instant, she had elegantly swept away the protection of the cloak with one hand and putting her fingers to her lips, whistled loudly and piercingly. Around twenty metres away her massive horse pricked up its ears and turned and ran towards her, sending two infantrymen sprawling on its way. Frighteningly large, it was an impressive sight thundering towards them in its protective armour. As it approached, Ségolène deftly grabbed the saddle with one hand and leaped up onto the horse's back, pulling two enormous swords from their sheathes on the saddle as she moved. It was absolutely artistic. She moved gracefully with fluid motion, every sinew acting together to create a beautiful, if violent, work of art.

The swords in hand she advanced on the first two hapless infantrymen as they tried to regain their footing, and with one on either side, taking two speedy swipes at each, they were down. Finn closed his eyes against the horrific sight as their heads rolled away in the opposite direction from their bodies, which stood as if bemused for a second, before dropping lifeless to the ground.

In another effortless single move she placed the swords back into their sheathes and drew a bow from across her back, pulled back on its drawstring and fired, not one but two arrows in marginally different directions, each hitting its target squarely in the forehead, in a gap in their badly designed headwear. A triumph of fashion over practicality, the helmets had been designed for ceremony and looking fearsome and menacing to the enemy, but having a fatal flaw, one that she took no hesitation in taking advantage of.

Still moving, she drew the swords and dispatched further infantrymen. The rest of them were panicked now and could hardly believe their eyes; this whirling dervish of a warrior attacking before asking questions and seemingly invincible. When a blow was made on her armour, it seemed to simply glance away as though she were not even there. They fled as she reached the phalanx, and stopped, laughing, as they went scattering in all directions. She headed back towards Finn, sheltered under his cloak, and then it began to rain, not raindrops but enormous stones. As if in an earthquake the entire face of the cliff seemed to be falling, and it was Finn's turn to act decisively.

He rushed forward and leaped up onto Ségolène's warhorse pulling the cloak over them as he moved. The rocks bounced off the protective covering and fell at their feet and those of her warhorse, and they were soon leaping over them, in the direction of the canyon opening, towards their enemy, who might be waiting beyond their sight. Ségolène whistled loudly again, and Finn's horse followed quickly behind. As they rounded the corner, true enough their assailants were there, waiting. They were much more reticent, however. Before Ségolène could react, a pack of rampaging wolves were racing towards them.

"We can't fight them off forever," shouted Finn, and Ségolène, grudgingly, acknowledged this.

"Get out your sword, Finn! Now!" Puzzled, he followed her advice. This puny sword in his hands was no match for the horde ahead. Ségolène brought her horse to a halt suddenly and threw him from it.

"Now raise the sword high above your head, and plant it into the earth as deep as you can. I'll do the rest!"

Finn again nodded in acknowledgement and proceeded to follow the instruction. He raised his sword high in the air, gripped firmly in both hands. He thought about what he was doing and with massive concentration stuck it firmly into the ground. Somehow, it easily penetrated the rock deeply, sinking in as if it were butter, and he felt an immediate surge of power from its hilt, making him release it in reflex action for fear of shock. He stood wide eyed looking at it as it appeared to grow, and he glanced up and saw that the snarlwolves were stopped in their tracks, concerned and confused by the sound which now emanated from it.

The ground was shaking and the infantrymen scattered once more, holding their ears to keep out the horrifying screeching noises now echoing around the canyon walls. More and more rocks were falling from the heights above now, and they were accompanied by men, their arms flailing wildly as they fell, and by strange monkey-like beasts, and more snarlwolves. Giant Ravens were hitting the side of the canyon and falling limp to the ground, buried in the rock fall.

Around Finn and Ségolène an area of safety seemed to exist, and the rocks fell to either side, the falling ravens bouncing off its invisible walls and into the line of fire of the falling rocks. Soon a swirling pit was opening up in the rock around the sword and the enemy fighters were being uncontrollably drawn into it. As they ran they were overtaken by the whirlpool and swallowed by it. The noise heightened and the screams of the soldiers joined in only to be drowned out by the rising tide of the clamour from the surrounding beasts. As the sounds came to a crescendo, a vicious wind rose up and captured the remaining enemy fighters driving them in the direction of the abyss, round and round in circles they went, down into the pit, into the depths into hell itself, for all Finn knew.

And then there was silence, except, momentarily, for the sound of the sword falling, clanking metallically to the ground, landing on the rocky outcrop it had been stuck into only moments previously. Finn wandered over to pick it up, and was horrified to hear a distant muffled screaming below the rocky surface, moving further from him with each second; the residual sound of the enemy army falling to their terrifying non-death. They might still be alive in there, and he wondered then just what Ségolène might do, what she was capable of, what horrors she might perpetrate, just to protect him.

And they were alone again, left to wonder how they had been tracked, and how they had been followed, and who might have done this to them. The answer was to be more shocking than Finn could possibly imagine.

20 *Arrival*

With the thrill over, a quiet, uneventful trip followed, thankfully. Back through the mountain foothills across the plain, they could feel the air changing of the feel of the Ocean approaching. Ségolène had started this stage of the journey, going over her battle, reliving its more memorable moments, as though committing it for future memoirs. She had become silent however when Finn failed to respond with appropriate enthusiasm.

"You're not really used to the carnage, are you?" she stated, obviously. "It's part of my world, not yours…it's kill or be killed here Finn, you have to realise, but you'll have to toughen up, if you are to fulfil your role. It won't be easy for you."

When he grunted some response, incoherently, she let it lie. Her role was protector, not a governess moulding his attitudes, his abilities, his feelings, and in a way she was thankful for this. She revelled in the fighting, it was clear, but motherly role building duties were anathema to her. She could empathise with him, but left it at that. Better keep the roles separate.

Time seemed to slow further as the journey's end approached. Soon they were riding along a sandy track, with white sand and slit fencing leading towards a seaside just as it had in Finn's youth. He remembered their visit to grand-dad's cabin at the beach; Finn and Dara running free along the sands, playing in pools and climbing rocks, and being young and free. No responsibility, no darkness, no fear, no enemies. They had each other and needed no one else. Best friends.

Soon in the distance a small township appeared, and they could smell the familiar ozone aroma of a windswept sea. Seagulls rose and dropped on thermals, enjoying their simple lives, waiting for their next free meal from the fishermen, who risked their lives daily to keep their village alive. The seagulls were ungrateful wretches who could never value the cost of the fish they stole.

The town was compact, neat and tidy, with a straight road leading down to the shore, and rows of wooden whitewashed houses, each constructed of carefully sawn planks of timber, with pitched roofs and shutters on the window holes. They had verandas, and each had a small flowerbed in the front, and vegetable patches out back. They did not seem to fit with mediaeval life and looked almost modern, or if not, 19th century. They certainly looked affluent.

Bearded locals, with Breton caps looked out from the verandas, sewing nets and smoking long clay pipes. They smiled cheerily at the passing warrior knights who felt totally self-conscious and out of time here. They kept straight on, waving back at the friendly natives, who seemed not the slightest perturbed at the weaponry dripping from the horses.

"Hello, young man," shouted a particularly old salty cove. "You'll obviously be looking for the Five Fathoms?"

"Yesss," answered Finn, concerned they knew his business.

"It's over there by the harbour. Your Father *will* be pleased to see you at last!"

"How do they know?" Finn asked his companion under his breath.

"They are obviously expecting you, somehow," she answered.

And there it was, the famed Public House; their destination.

"What concerns me," said Finn as he unpacked his things from the saddle roll, " is that my Mother made out I had to be secretive, keep it all hush, hush you know? Yet this lot seem to know all about me. It was supposed to be dangerous."

"Well let's go in and find out," Ségolène responded curtly.

It was a friendly looking place, painted a beautiful shade of duck egg blue, with a swinging sign denoting the Five Fathoms, in curly text. A badly drawn painting showed a shipwreck lying at an angle on the bottom of the sea, with its mast still visible thirty-three feet above, over the foaming surface. Atop the mast was a flag that was completely rigid. Or badly drawn. Finn recognised it immediately as his family coat of arms, the same one as on the roll protecting the map.

Entering through the swing doors, there was an overpowering smell of stale ale, rum, pipe smoke and cooking fish. Overall, it was vile. The interior of the main room was smoky and stained dark from years of abuse. Candlelight lit the room dimly and through the fug Finn could make out the bar area, and some tables. It was empty, devoid of life. He had expected it to be full, and to be making discreet queries about the whereabouts of his Father but here he didn't even know where to start.

"You'll find what you seek out in the back yard area, chopping wood," said a hidden voice, at which Finn jumped, making Ségolène become rigid and alert for a second, ready to hack down the dangerous owner of the voice. But the voice was a woman's; soft and sweet, with a hint of breathiness and a slight, subtle, lisp. Finn instinctively raised his hand as if to warn the warrior princess off any hasty un-necessary and violent move. Out of the shadows came a dark beauty, tumbling ringlets of blackest black hair; a black woman, the first Finn could remember seeing in this world.

"Thank you," he said quietly.

"He'll be pleased to see you, after all this time," she said.

"Which way?"

"Through that door…"

He walked through the door, expectant, thinking he would see a bronzed warrior, practicing his bodybuilding, chopping logs with an axe to keep in trim waiting for the call to arms. He was about to meet a King after all, and even if it was his Father, this was a moment of trepidation. Opening the door, the bright sunlight blinded him for an instant and he strained at the figure outside, which was drawn out long and sleekly thin through his squinting eyes.

"Ahh, Finn my boy," he said. "Made it at last!"

Ahead of him, a corpulent hairy naked torso stood, axe over his shoulder, head balding on top but with flowing locks down his shoulders and back, a huge bushy greying beard and an enormous smile. He threw down the axe and opened his arms for his son to run into. Finn blinked, but obliged and soon his arms were around the fat waist and he held him tightly as if he had not seen him for years. Tears filled his eyes and the exhaustion of the past few weeks suddenly engulfed him.

"Come on in. Tell me about your journey! I see you ended up with the assistance of my good friend, Ségolène. Thought she might come in handy. She's *very* handy with those swords, don't you think?"

"What's going on here, Dad?" asked Finn totally puzzled. " I've been sent here to get you. You are supposed to be in hiding, to be a secret. You need to come back with me and save the Homeland. Mum sent me to get you"

"Wait, wait, wait Finn," said his Father. "I'm through with fighting. Didn't your Mother tell you? I converted to Selfism. Miranda through there, you met her?,... is my guide. ... well, more my partner. I renounced all violence, all claim to the Crown, everything in fact. I don't need anything now."

"What? And does that include Mum?" Finn said with a hint of anger as it dawned on him what a waste of time this journey had been, and the fact that Dara was missing and hadn't even been found. And the fact that Dad didn't even seem to care. Perhaps he didn't know, though. It was incredibly confusing.

"No, no, no, Finn. She knows all about this. We arranged it. A little bit of training. A bit of an understatement that, but there you go. We had to take the risk, and get you away from that madman before he could really damage you. Like we sent you to the Other Place for safety. Look what happened there. Not too good an outcome. But well, that was an accident. Life's like that," he said dreamily gazing into space. Shaking his head he added, "Murchadh showed us how to do it before he disappeared. A trick he learned from our erstwhile friend's parent it seems."

"I suppose you should have known about my change of life. I just couldn't go on. The responsibility was too much for my shoulders. Needs someone stronger."

"And you mean - I'm that man; I'm stronger. I'm only seventeen you know!"

"Well, Arthurian legend from the Other Place says he was only fourteen. He did a great job, for a while. I read it in their books; saw it on the vision box thing. Prefer it here though; quiet, peace, the Ocean and sand and copious amounts of fish. Good for the soul."

"Oh and then there's the thing about Mum and me…she needs someone stronger too. We just took different paths. She likes the tradition, the rituals and the constitution. She needs the monarchy. It's in her blood. Me, I preferred the easy life. Working in this place, fishing, swimming, playing lute and loving my new girl. I do have some responsibilities you know. I run this entire town, they need me here, my organisational abilities, you know. And I have contacts," he nodded at Ségolène, winking once at her." Useful contacts who can protect them. Why do you think everyone is happy here?"

Finn felt a bit nauseous. This was not what he had come to expect. He was the messenger when he came into this town, and he was going to leave it as the vengeful warrior.

"Look, I was never going to bring peace to the Homeland. I wasn't the Light. You were the prophesised one. You can do it. Only you. You are your Mother's son, the leader of the Zephyrine. Chosen people. Chosen to rule, chosen to lead, by example."

"I can help, I can put you on the right track, like this journey. It's been tougher than I imagined it would be, you were lost to us at least once, but, look, it is transforming you. You are not the same boy who started. You have grown in stature, ability and attitude. You are on your way. You need to finish what we have begun. My life, my life is here now." And his head dropped in a sudden display of shame. He looked up, finally grabbed his son and hugged him.

"You think I don't grieve for you, for Dara. I don't know where he is, but there is a higher calling. Sacrifice has to be made."

Finn finally lost it.

"Sacrifice, sacrifice? Don't you care? What could have happened? Where might he be? And you shrug your shoulder and talk about sacrifice? What have you sacrificed, apart from your dignity. Look at you. Given up, fat, balding, taking the easy life when around you others are dying, and need you. Yes you. I'm too young; I'm not from here……… I can't do it!"

As he spoke, the wind gathered speed and the clouds swirled in the sky. His brooding dark thoughts became real, expressed in growing stormy weather. The clouds darkened and the gulls flew away squealing and hurriedly headed for safety.

"I can't do it!" he screamed out loud, and a bolt of lightning crashed at his Father's feet.

His Father was on his toes screaming in joy.

"Yes you can! Look at what you've just done!" He was dancing in triumph. His angry, brooding son had erupted in fury and brought down the elements on him. If he could do this he could face the greater enemy. His training was finished.

Ségolène smiled at him, proud as any Mother. And then he saw, somehow, in her face, that she was his Mother………

21 Return

Finn could hardly believe his eyes. These two individuals had merged as one person right before his blinking eyes. He rubbed them, but could not comprehend this. And then the illusion melted. His Mother was gone. He was now thinking, confused once more, if the trials of the past weeks had been for nothing, why had they risked his life, possibly killed Dara and brought him all this way on a wild goose chase?

He turned away trying to think. He walked towards the Five Fathoms, trying to fathom it out. Miranda met him at the door.

"He has waited for this moment for many years you know" she said quietly. "He is a great man; he is a great thinker, but he is not a great warrior. We are not all destined for greatness like you, Finn. He cannot do what has to be done."

"I know, because I hear him and feel him tossing and turning in his sleep, mumbling and muttering, troubled and worried with gnawing fear and frustration. He would go back if he could, but I would die. I cannot live without him and he knows it. Your Mother knows it too. There are things you cannot understand yet. But you will with time."

"You, and you alone, are our destiny. Only you can defeat him and bring peace to the whole land. Only you have it in you. You will know when it is time what to do because you are chosen. You have the mark of destiny, and you have the tools to do it. I should know because I chose you for it. When you were at death's door I was the one who was called, I placed my hands upon you and felt the power. I used my skills my ability and my alchemy to transform you from a sickly boy into a warrior. The blue stone I carry is in you. It feeds you, it gives you the power. I am Miranda, daughter of the sage and seer Murchadh. I carry his power into the future. I made you, and you will succeed because of the legacy of your parents and of the great Murchadh. You must go now. Time is of the essence."

Finn reeling with all the revelations spun round to see his Father and Ségolène arm around each other watching him from a distance. Care and concern on their faces. He then noticed for the first time the painting on the wall of an aged balding whiskery man, the one from the steps and from his dreams. A title plate under the frame read simply, Murchadh.

"We must hurry, Miranda, tell him all you can…time is indeed of the essence," said Evan McGarrigle.

"First and foremost, you need to get back to the Homelands, to Croí Dorchadas; the Heart of Darkness, so named because it is the heart of the darkness. It is the seat of pain and suffering. It may appear to be a happy joyous place, but inside it is rotten to the core. There is a secret in the

Castle; a secret you must destroy. It is the source of The Guardian's power." Finn nodded, speechless, waiting to find out his fate.

"We have mapped a route back to the Castle for you that you must follow; it flows past the New River. You must gather some of the water in this vial and keep it safe. On entering the heart of the Castle this water must be used douse the flame in the pit of the dungeons. This will extinguish The Guardian's flame, his power, and you will be able to defeat him once and for all.

The route we have chosen will help resolve your inner conflict. On the way you will experience the real reason we need him vanquished. Not only does he threaten peace in the Homeland and beyond, but also he is ravaging the earth in the name of his greed and his quest for power. The Mines of Moonstone lie on the route. His operations are polluting and killing the country. All is dying, and in its wake the quest for Moonstone will kill everything and everyone. He cares not for any of this. Only for his own power. You are our only hope. Go, now!" And as he finished, another new emotion crept across his face; excitement.

"One last thing though. You need a faster mode of transport than that you used to get here. Come with me"

His Father led him to a building at the rear of the Five Fathoms. Opening the double doors with a flourish, and a huge grin, his father revealed what lay beyond. Finn was greeted with a fantastical sight. In the darkness of the building, buried under piles of loosely strewn hay was what could only be described as a roman chariot! It was extravagantly impressive, white with golden embellishments. When it was pulled free of the straw, Finn could appreciate its true size, and the height of the wheels that seemed to tower over him. It had flames of crimson and blue and yellow emblazoned on the side, a true chariot of fire!

Miranda appeared from the rear of the building with two enormous white stallions, with manes of yellow, and they were dressed in the finest armour imaginable. It was elusive, so fine it seemed to be transparent, but it reeked of strength.

With the horses hitched up, and some supplies placed on the floor of the chariot, it was time for goodbyes.

"We will be looking out for you. You will not be alone. When the time comes you will know the power of this vehicle. Think, desire, and it should obey. Just be reasonable with it. It is, you will gather, alive and needs to be treated with respect. I think you will prosper my son. Now, you must go!"

And his Father slapped the closest white horse firmly on the rump. Finn grabbed the reins and it took off at fantastical speed. Looking back the Five Fathoms was soon a distant blip on the horizon.

With feelings of trepidation, he set forth to fulfil his still vague destiny. He knew a route had been set for him. He knew he was being led to the places he had to go. Obviously he was still learning, but the learning curve was getting steeper by the day and soon he would have to face up to the greatest test of his short life. But he felt confident.

The chariot felt as though it was flying and although close to the ground this did seem to be the case. The speed was exhilarating, and the countryside passed at an ever dizzying pace, trees seeming to bend as he flew, grass whipping as he crossed fields, towns a blur.

But soon, he was in open country and the earth here seemed scorched. Pockmarked and blackened it became increasingly polluted. There was little plant growth and he noticed that the towns he passed were devoid of life. On one occasion he thought positively, "Stop," and the chariot slowed and came to a halt. The village he entered was deserted. The buildings worn and distressed, places where life had teemed were now empty and silent and ghostly. On closer inspection he could see the remnants of life as skeletal remains littered the floors. He looked carefully around and saw this everywhere. Death stalked the streets and he decided it was unsafe to remain still.

Once again he was flying. The ground was black and lifeless. Oily residues filled what were once streams. It was vile and horrifying and he had a vision of how this might affect his Homeland if left unchecked. How could mining cause this destruction?

Soon he saw it; the mine. The horizon was hidden by the residual bings; mounds of spoil excavated and discarded as the mines were dug. They surrounded the mine workings and from these foul piles of excremental earth, streams of black and green puce emanated and flooded the surroundings. Burning fires filled the air with acrid smoke and the flames crimson and green, yellow and sulphurous, filled the air with a stench. The mine workings stretched as far as the eye could see.

Tiny ant like people scurried around busily working, pulling carts, breaking rocks, setting fires, smelting. Carpenters were building steadily a town that supplied the mines, in the midst of the pollution people were living and dying, and Finn could see this all laid out in front of him. The dead were left in the streets where they lay, the children played amongst them, the women gathered food and took water from the open wells Finn could hardly breathe, and used his cloak to provide shelter. He could see how the earth itself would die if this outrage were allowed to proceed unhindered, and knew he had to stop this living death.

After miles of pollution and stench and death, the countryside soon began to return to the lush, happy greenery of the Homeland. Then before him the New River appeared. It was a sight to behold. Wide and expansive, it was a brilliant turquoise green colour and radiated health and vitality, a ribbon of life winding slowly from the mountains and demanding his attention with its brilliant colour and fluid loose motion.

Taking the time to rest and feed, he tried to get the taste of the Minelands out of his mouth, but as they were now entrenched firmly in his mind this was impossible. Bread and cheese and starfruits. Simple things. He took the vial carefully in his hand and walked to the edge of the river. The water had a pleasing translucent opaque colouring. It wasn't transparent like most water, and when he put his hand into it, it felt beautifully silky to the touch. It also felt freezing cold, but then warm too, and it seemed to pulsate. It sparkled with vitality and life and cleared his mind of the misery of the mines. He felt wholly alive.

The vial filled, he stopped it and placed the vial in his bag, surrounding it with soft items like the cloak for protection. He accidentally fingered the deck of cards, lifted them from the bag and looked at them, and for an instant, he thought about throwing them away. From his hand, the pack slipped slowly into the running water and he felt an urgent need to rescue it them, as if they were crying out to him to be saved. He grabbed at them and shook off the water droplets and placed the pack back into his bag with the other items.

He was soon on his way once more, the vial safely tucked away in the bag, surrounded by a sheltering soft protective layer of cloak cloth. It was the most precious thing he had and he needed to keep it safe.

As if in a dream, the passing countryside passed at a normal pace, but he seemed to make incredible headway, as if time itself were being compressed. His experience was of normal time passing with the trees and road at his feet passing by at around ten miles per hour, but he seemed to travel much faster that that outside his immediate locus. Coming up to a copse on a hillside he blinked momentarily and it was suddenly gone; miles behind him now. Time and space seemed somehow to be warped and folded and it was getting him to his destination in double quick time.

The Castle appeared, forbidding and now menacing, on the horizon before he could realize it. Soon he was approaching the outskirts of the town; Home again. Finn swallowed and felt the fear rise as his head ached and the back of his neck tightened with tension.

He had a Man's Job to do and he had to grow up now. His childhood had slipped away without him realising it. Turning seventeen he had thought of himself as grown up, an adult. But he was still interested in toys, basically. He still had no responsibilities for anything, he could not feed himself, he could not find accommodation if he needed it. He didn't even know how to get a job. Even arriving here, the activities had been trivial and childish. Jousting in blue dress armour, running around the Castle dungeons, wandering about trying to foolishly outwit the dim servants. All these things were the games of a child, and now he needed to resolve himself and, basically, kill a man, before he was killed.

Fulfill a prophecy. How had that happened? And he seemed to have lost a brother on the way. The pain of that surged through him and his resolve cracked. How could he do it?

He remembered being taught about the dilemma faced by Shakespeare's *Hamlet* in English classes. "To be or not to be….?" The dichotomy, the indecision. The abject failure in the end, where Hamlet is paralysed by the indecision, and someone else has to step in and finish it for him. Is that how this would end? But he knew he had to get vengeance for what had become of his family, for what had happened to his brother, and for what would happen to his Land, if the mad tyrant got his way.

Here he was; Finn McGarrigle Lord High Protector of the Homelands. The enormity of the title now grew in significance, and he understood. He had been chosen, long before he knew it, long before anyone here was even born. He was the Protector, a Guardian angel, sent to deliver the land and its oppressed people from evil. It was biblical in proportion, and overwhelmed him. He knew he could succeed though. Everyone had faith in him. He had some charismatic protection that he could feel in the blood that pulsed through his veins. He felt strong and invincible, not in the way an ordinary teenager feels they are, but how an invincible warrior might. Vitality and strength radiated from him and he knew he was the Chosen One. He would succeed or die trying.

22 The Heart of Darkness

He arrived at the town and time returned to normal. The streets swept ahead of him and were lined by the ordinary townsfolk. They stepped aside as the warrior King returned to his kingdom, and many even bowed as the chariot passed majestically along swill littered roads, and headed on up the hill towards the Castle. The businessmen, aristocracy and bourgeois of the town followed suit. Doffing feathered caps they gave Finn implicit command of their lives. He was in charge, and they knew it. The time of finality was approaching.

The courtyard beckoned. It was worryingly empty. A few haycarts lay lazily around, some overturned as if by a squally wind. There was an air of desolation and neglect about the place, as if left to wrack and ruin. Flags and bunting from the tournament flitted around the courtyard, and litter blew around the site of his ritual humiliation those weeks, or could it have been years ago? A few horses wandered aimlessly in the near distance, eating hay which had been strewn across the yard from the abandoned carts.

Finn climbed down from his majestic transport, and walked to the door, carefully checking the bag was over his shoulder, strung on that slim, fragile, elusive strap. He put his hand into it as he walked and felt for the vial. Relief. It was there. Whole. Safe. Not leaking. And the cloak was there too, soft to touch but full of power and strength. And those damned cards. When this was over he would throw them away or try to learn the enigmatic game they had to be used for. Thinking positively, that was a good sign.

The door was open, blowing in the breeze, back and forward, banging in the wind. No tiny man, no Percival. Finn suddenly felt a pang of regret for not being nicer to the servants. They were only trying to help him. He would change this in future he decided.

The halls were cavernous and empty. It looked as though giant spiders had become squatters in the building and enormous filamentous silky webs were attached to all the walls. He hoped he would not come across any of their constructors. Small spiders were bad enough, but these must be monsters. He shivered and reached down to his sword for comfort. Head into the heart of the Castle, dead centre, into the dungeons. Find the fire. Concentrate, Finn…He walked with deadly slow precision, feeling his way instinctively to the seat of the power. How had he missed it before? It hummed in his head and pulsated.

Deeper and deeper into the labyrinthine Castle he walked, his palm flat against each door as he went, dismissing some and passing by, entering others as the hum pulsed through his fingers. Deep into the Heart of Darkness, the fear and anxiety increasing with each step, but resolve growing too. Water dripped from the walls now and he felt he was in the pit of the earth. It was as if he was deep in the mountain on which the Castle stood. Deeper than any one had ever been before. Even the men who had built this Castle seemed to have deserted it before this point. A Godforsaken place. Then, with a surge of pain in his head he knew he was there, the final door.

He placed his hand on the door handle and it burnt through his glove, he felt the searing heat as though it burnt right through the door. One final grab of the handle and the door cracked open; a strange light flowed out from the room and lit the darkness of the hall he stood in. It was a black light, which vanished elusively; not a warming, pleasing, cosy firelight, the type of light he knew from his Mother's cottage. There would be no happy gambolling shapes in this fire, he knew. He reached into the bag for the weapon of mass destruction, and found it.

"Hi Finn," said a familiar voice from the shadows, behind him. "We knew you would return, so all we had to do was wait." It was Dara.

Conflicting emotions filled Finn's mind. Dara was alive, but he was here; Why was he here? What was going on? And then the second figure emerged from the darkness, menacing dark and substantial. The Guardian. Things began to make sense.

"Hello, young Finn. I see you have returned, just as your very useful brother has predicted. I knew of course you would, but it helps even someone as influential and intelligent as me to have confirmation."

"My trap for you at the Gates was a miserable failure, I had thought. But then, I trapped a better catch, it seems."

Finn could see clearly that The Guardian was somehow wounded, he had a continual drip of blood, falling from a spot on his side, and he constantly shifted some dressing.

"Oh, I sense surprise. Well after you, or should I say your woman friend, beat off my little welcome committee in the mountains we thought it simpler to wait for you to come to us. Dara here has been a mine of information you know. Told me exactly where you were going. Very helpful, and he will of course be amply rewarded."

"Remember that role I had you pencilled in for? Well, it's been filled now, and I must say with a much more appropriate and grateful applicant. He will go far under my tutorage."

"Oh, yes, and that little irritating trick where I couldn't talk to you? Gone. It was tiresome, but with a little help from your friends nothing is insurmountable. It did involve a little act of betrayal of course, but why not keep it in the family?"

"Your Mother is in safe hands, for now, but her little magic tricks are at an end. Added to that, you might find it a touch difficult to return to the coast. Had a slight environmental issue; involved a lot of water and flames, I believe. Odd bedfellows, but very, very, effective."

Finn was dumbfounded, and unable to think straight enough to talk. The different directions of his thought lines created a total confusion in his head. Dara had betrayed him, his Mother and basically everyone. How could he do that? Where was everyone? Were they safe? And then his anger rose and he shouted at Dara, somewhat pointlessly, "What have you done?"

"It's always been the same old story, Finn," Dara replied quietly and controlled. "I have lived in your shadow, completely, for my entire life. When you suddenly become not only the heir to all this, but some sort of Messiah, then it all became too sickening. When we disappeared, I thought I had died, But you know what? This man, the one we all hated, rescued me, and he made me a promise. I will be you. I will have the power. Me, not you, and that all made complete sense to me. So, I told them where you might be found. Once I crossed that line, I went the whole hog. He knows the story. He knows you will kill him if you can. You are the Chosen One, but not for long…"

"I'll hunt you down and kill you once I get out of this," Finn said through gritted teeth. He was slightly panicked now as he did not know how to progress, but the answer seemed to be inside the door. He lunged forward and yanked the door open. He saw right into the Heart of Darkness. He looked into it and saw it was alive. Unbelievably there was on a platform in the centre of the room the revolving image of a large beating heart. It pulsated power throughout the room and his head felt as if it might explode. Jarring noises were all around and the room seemed to move, to shake, to reverberate as if the floor were on a constantly moving fault line, a crack deep into the earth.

A fierce heat scorched his face and he ducked in through the door and into the room, vial in hand, to face the immense power. The black light blinded him and he tripped as he crossed the threshold. In a slow, agonising, motion the vial went flying through the air. It twisted and turned, the liquid flowing up and down its length reaching for the surface furthest away from the flame. He reached out to grab it, to catch it, to protect it. But it was too late, and it smashed into a thousand shards on the stone floor. This had to be the end, he thought. They will come for me now. The bluish hued liquid drained out onto the floor, missing its target completely, and the flame burned on.

For a moment there was silence, but then the floor exploded into life. From a crack in the slate of the floor a dark chasm opened and the water came. Like its source, this vial produced an endless supply of water that surged into life and flowed out like a torrent. It whipped and sprayed and enveloped all in its path; turquoise liquid death to those unable to resist its flow. Finn was picked up on the current and washed out the door past the surprised faces of his enemies. They too were caught up in its violent flow. Rushing through the corridors, out of control, this river transported them up and out of the Castle, spewing them onto the ground as it entered the open space of the courtyard. Spraying out the door as if a fountain it began to fill the courtyard and overwhelmed the tiny fountain Finn remembered from his first night and the vision of Enid.

Finn shook himself like a wet dog, and leaped onto his chariot as The Guardian, also soaked to the skin, yelled hurried orders at a contingent of guards, now appearing from their cunning hiding places in amazement at the water flowing from the Castle doors. He saw that Dara appeared to be lying lifeless next to his new Master in the shallow but torrential stream, but this was not the time to check his pulse, and soon his body was flowing along with the current towards the portcullis.

"Get him!" The Guardian shouted. "I promise *not* to kill the soldier who captures that runt!" As one the group of screaming banshees hurtled out after him.

"And you, get my horse, NOWWWWW!"

Finn flew out of the gates and through the town, following the route of the river as it flooded through the entire town. Townsfolk were scattering and buildings flooding. No time to look now he headed out for the safest location. That old fool, Cyrill's, Boat on the edge of town.

Where better in a flood than a boat. The old idiot had been right all along. He had foreseen this, in a roundabout way. Finn laughed out loud. Even in the midst of failure he was positive. He had not yet managed to defeat The Guardian, and he was running for his life. He didn't know exactly what he would do when he got there, but it should be safer than staying here.

Regroup, plan, and think of a strategy. Looking over his shoulder, he could see that his assailants had become bogged down in the mire caused by the river of mystical water, but a solitary dot in the distance he knew to be The Guardian could be discerned easily. He could feel him coming.

Even at this distance he could feel his anger, the fury emanating from him like smoke from his nostrils. Well he would face up to him here in the open, at the boat at least. This would be on his terms, now.

Looming high above him the boat was in a state of near completion, and would obviously float. But there was still no water here. Cyrill ran out of his home next to the boat, a rough wooden shack, gesticulating at him to leave him be, get away from his precious boat, his life's work. It was for him alone. To save him for the future; a safe future away from the oppressive Guardian and any other bothersome people.

Finn stepped out of the chariot and stood feet apart waiting for the inevitable conflict. He had not the slightest idea of what to do, how to defeat this experienced warrior. Some quick clues from watching Ségolène were all he had, and his bag of tricks. He pulled out the cloak and felt for his sword, but they seemed inadequate. What to do, now?

The distant figure was getting larger, filling the horizon and growing with each gallop his horse made. Finn stood his ground, and in an instant the foe was in his sights. He took his sword from its sheath and stood firmly where he was. Inside, the turmoil was rising and he hoped the earth might simply swallow him, or the water would rush here and fill the valley drowning the psychotic Guardian, ending it once and for all. But he knew this wasn't going to happen.

He had to fight him; he must face him and win. He would only be the true leader, the Lord High Protector, when this had happened.

Cyrill fled the scene when he realised what was to transpire.

"Not as mad as you seem," thought Finn as he watched the wretch run for his life.

The Guardian seemed to be laughing manically as he arrived. He could hardly believe that this lone boy was going to take him on. Alone, he could dispatch this Pretender to his Crown once and for all and get on with his strategies and plans for the wider domination of the Homelands, and beyond. Nothing could stop him now. He leaped off the horse in one graceful move, and threw his cloak over his shoulder casually. He strode, assertively, towards Finn, and before Finn could do anything he had drawn his sword. In a fell swoop he swatted Finn's puny sword from his hand. The pain from the hilt being wrenched from his fingers surged up his arm and tears almost came.

"What do you think you are doing, boy? What did you think you could achieve? Against me? You are nothing, and I will simply put you down like a mad dog," and he went to strike Finn with the sword. Finn used the cloak to deflect the blow.

"Ah, it's sport you're after? I think I can indulge, for a short time. It will be more… satisfying…," The Guardian said with a twinkle of malice in his eyes, and a slight grin under the moustache. "Pick it up," he said, and he gestured at the sword on the sandy ground with his own.

Without turning away Finn leant down and picked it up. Before he had a chance to raise it in anger he was blasted from his feet by a burst of energy flowing from the tip of The Guardian's sword. There was manic laughter, once more.

"This will be more fun than I thought. You will need an army to defeat me, BOY!"

High above him clouds began to mass and swirl, and lightning bolts lit the darkening sky. Finn tried to stand. But another bolt of energy sapped his strength and he fell to the ground.

"Do you really think these amateur theatrics are any match for me!" The Guardian shouted, and fired energy from his sword high up into the sky, which began to clear.

In desperation Finn grabbed a handful of sand and threw it directly at The Guardian's face. This old simple trick worked and gained him enough time to stand once more.

"Very good!" shouted The Guardian, blinking and clearing the sand from his eyes " I never knew you had it in you!" But he let go another energy blast and this time Finn was lifted high in the air and landed on the deck of the ark.

This seemed a mistake to Finn, once he had controlled the pain and stood up. He now had some cover. But The Guardian was climbing the scaffolding, his lean long body effortlessly ascending the rickety temporary structure. Finn knew he would be climbing, and occasionally peaked over the edge, avoiding lightning bolts, to see where he was.

"It's not very sporting," he shouted, " to use that thing."

More laughter. Finn grabbed the rail of the prow and jumped over onto the scaffolding. Kicking the ties, and cutting with his sword, he detached the scaffold from any permanent mooring it might have had. Using the prow for purchase, he used both legs on the scaffolding and pushed with all his might. It started to move, and in seconds it was toppling. Forming an arc, the scaffold fell to the ground taking The Guardian with it. He landed awkwardly, and the sound of his leg breaking could clearly be heard. He still had a dangerous weapon in his hand, though, and aimed it up at Finn who was now hanging from the prow. He too fell as the energy lashed him, screaming in agony.

The Guardian was on his feet, and even in the agony of his broken leg he dragged himself across the sand towards Finn, who lay winded on the ground. Finn was sure this was the end. The Guardian, exhausted stood above him, sword in hand waiting to plunge it into Finn's defenceless body. Finn scrambled in panic for some weapon and reached into the bag that had miraculously stayed with him. All he could find was the useless pack of cards. Defiantly he grabbed them out of the bag and flicked them all into The Guardian's maniacal twisted face.

"Try this: it's fifty-one card pick up!" he screamed, and confused and in a tongue he had never spoken before, added " Ardghar er ertuma!"

The Guardian's face changed to bemused as he batted the flying cards away. He lifted the sword higher as if to finish Finn off with a flourish. It began to glow. But the look on The Guardian's face changed once more, for before he had time to act, he saw that the cards, as each one individually hit the ground, metamorphosed into a grotesque person; sand people erupting from the ground below his feet, grabbing at him and pawing and clawing. A whirlwind of sand whipped up around them. Their faces were twisted in the agony of their rebirth, their appearance from paper death and they looked as though they needed some succour to feed them at this birth. Sand flowed out of their mouths, nostrils, and eye sockets The Guardian was completely engulfed in the twisted clamouring faces, and they dragged him down; deep down into their midst.

Finn was screaming in fear, concerned that they would turn on him. Where had they come from? He hadn't yet registered that they were emanating from the cards on the ground. Soon all fifty-one had appeared, their bald angry heads screaming silently and blinking in the sunlight, blinded by a daylight they had never experienced before. They climbed over one another to get up to that light and dragged The Guardian down into their midst, standing on him and clambering over each other. Soon he was invisible under the pile of grey flesh, shining billiard ball heads and black sightless eyes.

He could be heard screaming in amongst them, but couldn't be seen. And suddenly the screams stopped and silence took over. On that cue, the writhing mass began to dissolve and shrink and disappear back into the sand, from whence it had come, and in a minute there were only the cards left, toppling and blowing over on the breeze. No sign of the tyrant; no body, no sound, nothing but the silence.

Finn was lying on his back, his elbows on the ground raising his upper torso to see what was happening. He kicked at the sand at his feet, but there was nothing. Silence, except for the sound of the wind whistling through the timbers. Shaking in terror, he stood and began to gather himself. Then he noticed there was something; The Guardian's sword. He walked over and picked it up, and for the first time appreciated the beauty of the weapon. It felt exactly right in his hands, the weight, the balance, and the strange elegant lightness of it, for a sword so massive.

Turning it over, the sunlight glinted on its blade and light flashed in all directions, it hummed, then died. There was the comfort of the leather hilt in his hand. He examined the sword and saw faint writing on the hilt. It was his initials, and the coat of arms that had been on the wrap around the map. This was his sword. How obvious now. He tried to will it to work, but there was no surge of energy, no electricity, no power. But it was still a powerful, balanced, but ordinary sword. He stuck it into his belt and thought about the sheath it might have some day soon.

"So you lot were useful after all," he said out loud to the cards, as he began to pick them up. As he did, he counted, just to make sure he got them all. Who knows how useful they may be in the future? Strangely, there was one extra. A full deck of fifty-two cards.

Finn set about heading back into the town. He approached the first buildings and noticed the muddy residue in the streets, but no river. Slowly, he rode his chariot up the streets towards the Castle. There was no throng lining the streets, no triumphant welcoming party.

A party of dejected soldiers wandered dazed and confused. Whatever hold The Guardian might have had over them seemed to have dissipated with his demise. They seemed unsure of where they were, or what they were doing, and at least one looking in his direction, nodded a greeting. As he progressed slowly through the mud he noticed the bodies of thousands of rats, which he assumed had been spewed out of the Castle basements with the torrent.

"Sire," a voice in a doorway shouted. " How can we help?" An armed guard was looking around at the destruction, and needed direction.

"Gather those men back there, and start searching homes. Ensure there are no casualties. Report back to me at the Castle. I will plan as I go. What is your name? Do you have a rank? Have you experience in leading groups?"

"I am Darcus Flange, infantryman and Castle guard. I simply know that you need help here. We need to rebuild, starting now. Some of my compatriots have fled. But I can muster enough to start the work in hand."

"Then, Darcus, as you have shown some initiative, you will be my personal contact with your military friends." He threw him his skean dubh with the coat of arms emblazoned on its sheath, below the Celtic symbols, etched is silver.

"Use this as badge of office; like my business card if you like," he said to the perplexed soldier." Go on, there is too much to do, to stand about talking. Come and see me this evening. We will talk about strategy."

The soldier set off looking for comrades and began organising rescue parties. Finn continued up the hill, wondering where the water had gone. As he entered the courtyard he expected to find a lifeless body waiting for him. His treacherous brother Dara. But when he got there, there was no one to be seen. An oily, rotund figure rolled into view. Percival.

"My Lord I see you have returned. Sir Dara has departed, my Lord. He said to inform you of his sorrow, his shame and contrition. He will not return. His eyes have been opened, he says but what he did was too much to bear. You will not see him again. I believe that was the message."

The surge of emotion filled the courtyard and Finn grieved for his Lost Brother there and then, in a scream of agony that filled the air for miles. Pulling himself together he entered the sodden building, looking at the ruined interior and the general devastation.

"Get this cleaned up," he said in utter dejection, and he made his way to the banqueting hall, where he knew his throne would be, vacant. He sat in it and thought long and hard.

He could no longer feel the hum of the fire in the heart of darkness now, and surmised evidently that as the water in the room rose, it had extinguished the flame. But the power of the flame must have annihilated the source of the water. It could be destroyed after all.

He sat wondering who was still alive, where everyone was, and what he would do; now he was no longer just High Lord Protector, but a King. But he knew he would think of something.

23……After

With the ruins of Watersedge and the Five Fathoms rebuilt from their ashes, and his Father installed in his capacity as local ambassador, Finn took his first Journey from the homelands since the fateful events. He recounted to the assembled family, how he was dealing with the problems left in the wake of The Guardian's demise. His Father had been seriously injured in The Guardian's evil revenge. He, now, was the man in a wheelchair, designed by Finn, and wheeled around by his faithful Miranda, who was totally unscathed in the attack, the benefit of being a witch, Finn surmised.

In a slightly bizarre, and uncomfortable, twist, his Mother had moved there too.

"To benefit from the sea air," she had said.

So a full family meal was possible. They included the exiled Dara in this. An empty place was set at the meal, just in case he appeared. They all regarded him as some sort of victim in this too, and vowed to try their best to welcome him should he return. Ségolène was honoured too and they explained she was assisting the Tree people rounding up The Guardian's final loyal brigade, now hunted outlaws, hiding in the forests of the Wastelands, or in caves and holes by the Great Canyon. Few remained, but as long as there was one, they would be hunted down.

Finn had literally cleaned up the town and reinstated a Government. His role was advisor and figurehead. He ruled benevolently, but tried to keep to the back seat. He had no idea what a true ruler should do. Responsibility was delegated to his Government, under the leadership of his good friend, Darcus Flange. The colossal army were occupied in rebuilding the Kingdom; a contingency was kept employed transporting Cyrill's titanic boat to the sea. His first ship in a navy he had planned. What lay beyond the seas? He hoped to find out.

More importantly for the peace of the joint nations he immediately put a halt to the fighting on the Battlefield of Lyre. No one could remember what the fighting was for, so why continue? This was not surrender; it was triumph, a chance to save a generation of doomed youth. As the Homeland army retreated, still under a rain of flaming lanterns, Finn rode majestically into the no mans land in the centre of the battlefield, protected by his cloak, of course, and had signalled to the enemy. The fight was over. His defiant stand brought the two sides together and in the discussions that followed it was evidently true that no side knew what the war was about. It was simple to gain agreement on armistice. The war was over and the soldiers went back to their homes, no wiser. With no leadership the enemy had been fighting with no direction and no knowledge of their reasoning. It was a futile battle. Now over. Finn's leadership was assumed and the entire continent became his Kingdom, his responsibility.

Next, he had commenced to tackle the environmental disaster at the moonstone mines. Closing these down and plugging the mineshafts to prevent the Blue Moonstone corrupting others and causing further widespread pollution, he set the redundant workforce the task of repairing the evident damage their work had caused.

Growing daily in stature, Finn was now the ruler of all the lands. His previous miserable life forgotten, he had fulfilled another part of his destiny. He brought his wife Enid with him to join the family in celebration. She still could not speak to anyone but him, and he understood implicitly every thought she had. They were as one in mind.

One tale Finn did regale them with regarded the deck of cards. He needed advice, or rather comfort that he had handled a situation properly. He told his Mother how the cards had come to his rescue in his hour of need and how they now numbered fifty-two, but still seemed not to be a full deck. Each was different after all. To knowing looks he stated his theory that their dip into the River of Life, as he had rechristened it, had somehow brought them to life, just in time to save him. His Mother nodded, sagely.

"I am afraid I set that one up for you. I knew you would look at the cards just that once more, and, of course, just at the right location. It was obvious you would try to get rid of them, but you heard them call out to you. The River simply rejuvenated them. They were waiting all along to help you."

Finn continued that he had noticed a strange effect in the newest card. It had begun slowly to darken at the edges, and a sepia tinge had infused through it within a matter of days. Weeks later, it was black as night, and the outline of the figure trapped in its core was barely visible. Finn had thought carefully about how to deal with it, and his instinct told him it was not a good idea to retain it within the deck. The fact that several others had begun to change colour around their frayed edges also concerned him. He consulted with his friend Darcus and together they decided to separate this card from the rest.

Using sugar tongs to avoid touching it, they placed it carefully in a glass box, which Finn had crafted specially for the purpose. The idea would be they would be able to inspect it for any further changes without having to handle it. Together, Darcus and Finn had ventured back into the depths of the Castle to the room containing the Heart of Darkness; the most secure location they could think of, and the one only they now had access to. The flame had been relit and appeared benign now, and would give them effective light to assess the image on the card when they had to, without introducing any further light source; who knows what might affect the card? For safety, they threw the tongs into the flame and a flash of blue light emanated then died.

Away from its influence, the other cards had returned to normal, and with daily inspection the lone card appeared to lighten slightly. The inspections soon became weekly and then monthly, with no change to the appearance of the card. Safely hidden away, the box contained the secret.

After careful consideration of this strategy, Finn's Father concluded this was the only possible solution. They couldn't destroy the card, as they didn't know what effect this would have, so keeping it close to their chest, as in a real game of cards was an ideal solution. If only the two confidantes and his family knew of its whereabouts and its true nature, then all would be safe. What could possibly go wrong?

As the meal was concluded, and he left, he looked back at the blue timbers of the Five Fathoms and wondered whether his Father's lazy life of peace was better than his full life, leading a country. As before, he still felt like a fraud. He didn't ever know what he would do next, but he always thought of something, or knew someone else who could.

Later

The sound of a car horn woke him from reverie with an annoying start, and his daydream of mystical times. He was on a busy street in a large city, and it was a blisteringly hot sunny day. Leaves rustled in trees as a bright breeze whistled through them. Looking down at his legs he shifted them with effort, but he knew he had to avoid sores. The resentment of his plight had gone with the adventure; with time. He felt confident now and nothing could change his mood. He was dressed in the best black suit he could imagine. It felt wonderful, as smooth and soft as silky wool. The tailoring was superb and the suit fitted him like a glove. The shoes were the finest Italian leather, soft to the touch of his hands and would be just the right support to the high arches he couldn't feel, as thought made to measure. Still only nineteen, he felt a million dollars in these clothes, and strode tall, even in the chair. He wore an assertive but knowing smile, and felt like he was on top of the world, on top of his game and at the height of his powers. And his hair was perfect.

Across the street was a small church, and he became aware that he had an appointment, some requirement to enter it. He pulled out purposefully through the parked cars and the traffic seemed to part for him. He was invincible like all teenagers and could cross roads in front of traffic with impunity. A crowd gathered at the darkened doorway and he seemed to know them all. No one talked but they all looked down at him with compassion in their eyes, smiling forcedly, with an air of understanding, as he walked towards them. No words were spoken. He sailed through the crowd as though they did not exist and entered the vestibule. Another small huddled group, mixed sex he noticed, and mostly his age were gathered here and there, and they too looked at him as he sailed through, eyes following his back, he felt.

The church was tiny, with a vaulted roof with a small dome in the centre. It had the most magnificent stark black and white tiling around the walls and above the rows of pews were sandstone plaques dedicated to the great and good. Many of them seemed to show fallen heroes; warriors of two Wars, with the occasional saintly do-gooder, or inventor, or composer, or poet amongst them. He reeled them off as he passed each one, clicking an imaginary counter as he rolled. One ancient tablet in particular caught his eye.

'IN DEDICATION OF OUR DEAR BROTHER AND SISTER
EVAN & CAILIN M'GARRIGLE
FOR THEIR ENORMOUS SACRIFICE
IN THE HOMELAND WARS'

Then there was a space, and some text added later in a different hand;

'AND THEIR SON, DARA'

Finn seemed not to recognise the significance of the names immediately, and sailed on arrogantly and assertively into the centre of the church. Then, even though aware of his parent's names on the plaque, he blithely ignored it, couched in a feeling of satisfaction. They were a success. They sacrificed themselves for a better life for others, for a cause, and they were commemorated for it. What better tribute could there be? A plaque, here, commemorating your life and its outcome. Immortality, in stone.

He found his way to a seat at the front and soon music began. A church organ played loudly Bach's *Toccata and Fugue*; so familiar with its staccato, stops and plain loudness. It was like rock music from the 18th century. Finn remembered it being used in a film his Dad had made him watch. '*A Canterbury Tale.*' It was in black and white and made during the war, and he pretended to be bored witless, but had watched intently.

"A bit of culture," Dad had explained. "It's about life in wartime, I'm sure you'll like it, if not now some time in the future."

Strangely, the images came back to haunt him occasionally. He still thought about the Second World War frequently and what it must have been like, particularly in the South of England. All that uncertainty, all the threat; glamourised monochrome images filled his head with Spitfires and Lancaster bombers and moustachioed pilots with unspeakably upright accents and a devil may care attitude. He found he watched WWII films when he had the chance, and immersed himself in the history, but only superficially. He didn't really want to know the real horror, not at his age.

When the *Fugue* passed away, Elgar's '*Nimrod*', slow and solemn and profound, replaced it. In turn, this was followed by Holst's *'I vow to thee my country'*. They all seemed appropriate, and to his liking. Just right for the ceremony. Ritual. These were important pieces of music, timeless and deep, influential. They were closely associated with war and remembrance and resonated through his life.

He remembered them on the HiFi, his Dad replaying them in solemn moods, on the TV when the remembrance ceremony was on in November, for Armistice Day, or played with more brassy exuberance by an RAF band which came to the school. He was sure he would hate it, but again he was surprised by the intensity of the music and the effect it had on him. It took him into the fantasy of living in a balmy 1940's wartime summer, bees buzzing around and daisies on the airfield, a camp chair and the men twirling moustaches and smoking pipes. Expectancy of something happening. The long boredom followed by the adrenalin rush of scrambling. He was living in black and white, and in a different life. He found himself lost in the depth of the music, still too youthful though now, to appreciate the real intricacies of it or its solemn virtues.

Languidly, as though not wishing to be seen to eager to enter, the crowds assembled in the pews, and Finn found himself at the front of a throng. There was a silent chatter amongst them, but he understood none of it. He could not remember anyone talking to him since he arrived. And he still did not recognise a soul.

A man in a pale suit appeared before him, carrying a suit of chain mail, a brown tattered tunic and a sword, sheathed in black leather, its hilt worn and frayed. He laid them ceremoniously on to a small dais in front of the congregation, and walked backwards respectfully away from them, his head bowed in what seemed to be sorrow.

There was a jarring accidental chord from the organ, a shouted apology from stage left, and then a more soothing sustained note (G it so happened, for Finn recognised this as a favourite of his Dad's, the long introduction to Pink Floyd's *Shine on You Crazy Diamond)* and the assembled crowd soon stood as one, leaving Finn, embarrassingly slowly, missing the beat and obviously the last to stand. The stirring sound was replaced by silence and then a young elfin woman appeared on the raised platform next to the clothing before him. She smiled directly at him, and blinked away a small tear. A man appeared and began to speak.

"Friends, Brothers, Sisters. My name is Dr Walter Kissling." (He strongly emphasised the V at the start of Walter)

"My life has been dedicated to the study of the man we celebrate today. I would give up my life for him were he to ask. If only he were to. We gather here today to celebrate the life of a true and singular hero. To eulogise; to commemorate the saviour of the Homelands, to whom we are eternally indebted and whom it is said passed away exactly Seven Hundred and Seventy Seven years ago, this very day, at Eight Seventeen on the evening of the Seventh of July. The records left by him state clearly how the date shall be carried forward, and he even foresaw the change from Julian to Gregorian calendars, such was the great foresight of our Lord and Master, thus allowing us congregation at the correct and auspicious time."

"When the world was in its darkest hour; when all around had failed, betrayed or deserted us, one warrior rose from the ashes of defeat and protected the Homeland and freed the people that they could live in peace! You, the gathered and true descendants of this colossus of men can lay claim to being the true keepers of the flame, The Guardians of truth and the protectors of all that is good in this world. Without Finn McGarrigle," (he gasped as if he had not guessed this display was in his honour) "…this world would be a dark deadly place, haunted by the deeds of the evil doers, the despicable, murderous and vile defilers of truth and beauty, eternally living in darkness and hate and fear. I raise a toast to our saviour - Finn McGarrigle, Lord High Protector of the Homelands. May he live eternally in our memory!"

Ripples of muted, polite applause greeted the crescendo of praise. Finn felt as though the world was his. He beamed at the elfin girl, and thought of whom she reminded him, but that seemed very long ago now, when he was young and brave and Lord of all he surveyed. But that was such a long, long time ago. Why had he thought that? He felt weary now, but watched the crowd as they joined in celebration of him, but not him, for this was someone else from mediaeval times. He stood to join them but found himself unable to, his legs having crumpled beneath him. Tired, he sat and watched as the joy enfolded.

He soon began to smile again and he saw that this was a celebration not of him now, but him then. So how or why was he here? The Spirit of Finn, not the substance. He was here to experience the eulogy, the praise and the thanks, and to see the world he created many, many, years hence as he had written in prophecy in those dark defeated days……………..

"Go forth and spread the fire. Tell all you meet of his deeds!" shouted Kissling, joyously, as if with religious fervour, and the crowd dispersed through to the streets; a secret society of his own making, his descendants, his legacy, his future. And then, alone in the empty church, the elfin girl approached him. The only one to do so. She reminded him so much of Enid, but she could not be, not here; not now in this time.

"They are mere mortals, Sire, they cannot see you, as I can. Do not allow that to worry you. My ancestors gave me the gift. You too are mortal, or were once. And you too are my ancestor." She whispered into the back of his mind, as if not speaking.

"This celebration, it is a reminder to them that you are never far away. And that you will return; but only when they need you most. They do not see you, but they know you are there. Protector, after all has to mean something."

She raised her palm to her lips and blew a shimmering dust from it, and disappeared in the cloud it left. Alone again, he stepped from the chair without effort and turned to leave, but the doors slammed in his face with a resounding echo. As he turned to the look back into the church, on the floor in the nave ahead he caught sight of it; the tombstone bearing his coat of arms, and he was once again at peace.

To be continued….

Stephen P Burns was born in Dumfries in South West Scotland. He has lived in various locations in Scotland and Ireland, and recently moved with his wife and two boys to the inspirational Okanagan Valley in BC Canada in search of a new life. He has no dogs.

Finn's Destiny: The Hand of Fate is his first Novel.

Made in the USA
Charleston, SC
29 August 2010